MW01674929

The Home of the Heart

SALZWASSER
VERLAG

Miss Aird

The Home of the Heart

Reprint of the original, first published in 1863.

1st Edition 2022 | ISBN: 978-3-37500-216-9

Verlag (Publisher): Salzwasser Verlag GmbH, Zeilweg 44, 60439 Frankfurt, Deutschland
Vertretungsberechtigt (Authorized to represent): E. Roepke, Zeilweg 44, 60439 Frankfurt, Deutschland
Druck (Print): Books on Demand GmbH, In de Tarpen 42, 22848 Norderstedt, Deutschland

THE HOME OF THE HEART:

AND OTHER POEMS,

MORAL & RELIGIOUS.

By MISS AIRD,

KILMARNOCK.

> " The sounds, the strains of Truth that start,
> Spontaneous from the glowing heart,
> To other hearts resistless glide ;
> 'Tis *Truth* alone that sanctifies
> Song's sweetest, rudest harmonies ;
> *We pray* that *these* be sanctified."

KILMARNOCK

MDCCCLXIII.

TO MY FRIENDS.

"My early friends, friends of my evil days,
Friends in my mirth, friends in my misery too,
Friends given by God in mercy and in love!
My comforters and counsellors, my guides,
My joy in grief, my second bliss in joy,
Companions of my young desires, in doubt
My oracles, my wings in high pursuit!"

AND to my friends of every class—rich and poor, titled and talented—who have honoured me with their names as subscribers, these few stray leaves are gratefully and respectfully dedicated—gathered by the hand of a tenderly sympathetic friendship, to relieve "the feeble pulse and languid limb" of that sense of inactivity oft shadowing the heart with weariness, when cast into the golden crucible of affliction. And now, placed in the crystal of table-talk, neither "to assert nor claim a poet's name," with

"No design,
To make the pitiful possessor shine;
To purchase, at the fool-frequented fair
Of vanity, a wreath for self to wear." But strewn
"Like wild flowers on the pilgrim's way,
To cheer, but not protract his stay."

Not to speak high oracles—for exotics they are not—more the resistless impulse, the natural overflowings of sympathetic feeling, seeking expression in simple rhyme, than the studied effort of matured and cultivated thought. Written at a common hearth, by a common hand, moving more frequently to the dictates of circumstance than taste,—fostered on no classic ground,—almost the exclusive fruit of self-culture, and not a little self-denial,—unmeasured by the "clock-work tintinabulum" of prosody, therefore no spirited distillations, analyzed in the refining alembic of orthography. But "a friend must bear a friend's infirmities"—"despise not then the wild flower—small it seems and of neglected growth"—and who would crush the tinniest weed, that cheers with green a lonely spot. My classic friends will forgive my presumption, and cast the salt of Christian charity into whatever *in them is bitter*, when they know I have never written a single verse by measure, nor a sentence by rule—my Bible being my only lexicon. Seeing "I know not *Grecian* letters, having never learned," neither studied nor imitated, save unwittingly, any known author, nor tried to write an immortal poem—though *I have written for immortality*—and therefore they *may* be *weak*, *foolish*, and *despised*, to him familiar with "verse in the finest mould of fancy cast,"—

"Whose musical finesse is such,
So nice his ear, so delicate his touch,"
That nature's dew is stale when not Castalian,—

I crave from him what I have sought from Heaven—forgiveness. May they leave on every mind they offend what the vessel leaves on the wave; and may He who despises not the day of small things—"who never *dooms* to *waste* the strength He deigns impart"—"separate the precious from the vile, that I may not darken counsel with words without knowledge." Whatever is mine may He blot—let them be but the "wool" in which His own scripture jewellery is wrapt. In the sanctuary balance they may be hay and stubble,—in themselves they are nothing, less than nothing, and vanity.

The motive sanctifies alone the deed,
  Be it the seal that characters the thought,
And stamps the impress of the Spirit's meed,
  In value though the offering be as nought.

For good, not evil, is my *one* talent cast *conscientiously* into the *public treasury*. I see, lettered by the same hand that stamps His image and superscription on the ten of the more gifted, "Occupy till I come." Believing that there is no sex in soul;—that the powers of this little embryo spirit are formed and destined to unfold for ever,—that its every attribute evolves the design of indefinite cultivation,—that intellectual and spiritual progression are its birthright—born to bud and expand by approximation, and rise in fragrance for ever towards the perfection of its Author,—who will deny me the exercise of its influence, however mean? Shall I hide my Lord's money? Its appeal is to a higher audit than human opinion, though that I despise not. The blind eye of prejudice may frown on what the eye of Heaven looks kindly. And where is the leaf, however lowly, on which the dew of heaven may not fall. To the querulous, "such philosophic stuff" may prove nothing; to his jaundiced eye,

> "The primrose by the river's brim,
> A *yellow* primrose is to him,
> And it is nothing more."

For such I have but one sentence,—I "write injuries in sand, but kindnesses in marble." Give me then, as an honour and a privilege, a seat by your hearths, that I may win for the truths these home-spun lays are emulous of commending, "a Home in the Heart." "If I get not the heart, I get nothing—that which does not affect is soon forgotten." The affections are the palate of the soul—the golden key to the palace of thought; let but a word touch, with its spirit-breath, these chords that make "the music of humanity," and some tender string, true to our common nature, and thrilling with a thousand associations, in tones of gentle sympathy, will vibrate with its "touch of kin." It may be a wandering note from some old melody—a mother's song on the home-sick exile's ear. In "the ballad he learned at her knee," fresh in "the light of other days," the lava of the heart restores her buried dead—conscience stirs beneath the ethereal presence of thought, when memory weeps over her darkened pictures. And though dim with many a tear and sin, cold and still as monumental marble, the prodigal spirit returns from the solitudes of a broken trust, and, beneath the spirit-workings of a diviner influence, melts into the embrace of holier likings.

Stealing, unseen, like wind along the sea,
The "still small voice" of gentle charity,
More in its echo than its utterance lies,
"The still sad music of humanity,"
Eats into stony hearts through tears and sighs.

Though poetry is not piety, nor religion sensibility, every Christian, in a certain sense, is a poet. Through the angel-tongue of worship, soft, in the bosom of his God, the saint his spirit pours. To him the temples of nature and revelation are redolent of poetry; and the manna of its golden-pot is hidden to those who, forgetting *one* end of their being, have not learned to read its language of similitudes—helping, by things which are seen, the eye of Faith, in glorious figure, "to take a glimpse within the veil." Let no man, therefore, call that *class* of composition commen or unclean, which the Eternal Spirit has consecrated as the immediate medium of Divine revelation. God has voiced his will, and uttered the memory of His great goodness, through the sublime poetry of type, symbol, prophecy, and parable,—descending on that presence-cloud, to illumine with the brightness of His glory our sin-darkened world, and commune, in words of peace, with man.

"Though few may hear, and fewer heed my strain,
Yet Truth alone, where'er my lot is cast,
Shall be my chosen theme—my glory to the last."

"Would they were worthier!" and the glory and wisdom of all they

"Dictate this the drift,
That man is dead in sin, and life a gift."

BIRTH-DAY AND BRIDAL SONG, ON THE RIGHT HON. THE EARL OF EGLINTON AND WINTON'S MARRIAGE WITH LADY SOPHIA PELHAM.

TUNE—"*Scots wha hae.*"

WAVE the purple banner high!
Shoot the rocket in the sky!
Boom the cannon joyously,
Round Castle o' Montgomerie!
Festal garlands arch the way,
To welcome Lord and Lady gay;
With mirth and music crown the day,
The Birth-day o' Montgomerie!

Woods and waters softly sing;
Bells from tower and castle ring;
Hall and cot, your beauty bring,
To greet *our* Lord Montgomerie!
Through the woods let echo call
Evergreens to deck the hall;
Roses, lilies, gather all,
To crown the *Bride* Montgomerie!

The Thistle and the English rose,
That "now in noble union" grows,
Long may they live "afar frae foes,"
In Castle o' Montgomerie;
From east and west, auld Scotia's pride,
In beauty gather, side by side,
To greet the Bridegroom and the Bride,
In Castle o' Montgomerie!

Now, Irvine, sing a silver song,
Your green and flowery banks along,
While crowds of gallant nobles throng
The Castle o' Montgomerie!
And o'er the broad domain be sung
The joy of Lord and Lady—one;
Our ancient House of Eglinton,
Now "Pelham and Montgomerie!"

CONTENTS.

THE

HOME OF THE HEART.

THE HOME OF THE HEART.

"These lands in their garniture are bright,
But I know of a land where falls no blight."

Tell me, sweet, if free to roam
O'er earth, what clime would'st make thy home?
Are there no spots on her flowery breast
Where thou could'st make a lasting rest?
Flowery glade and shining stream,
Bright as thine own, in beauty gleam.
There are richer fruits 'neath sunnier skies,
Birds bright-plumed in a thousand dyes,
Where the breeze is rife with rich perfume,
Exhaled from flowers of gorgeous bloom;
Where earth is decked like a festal hall,
When the golden shadows of autumn fall.
Would'st dwell in lands more bright and fair
Than the stormy north—then tell me where?

Would'st dwell where the pale-leafed lote-trees blow,
And the ring-dove's notes are soft and low;
Where the silver tones of the mango bird
In forests of cadma trees are heard;
Where golden clusters of champae flowers
Enwreath the rich verandah bowers;
Where groves of acacia ever bloom,
And the earth, when pressed, exhales perfume;
Where Ganges rolls his broad, bright wave,
O'er the gold and gifts of the idol-slave;
Where superstition piles the pyre
For the devotee, in her tomb of fire;
"Where birds the hues of the rainbow wear"—
Would'st dwell in that land?—"Not there! not there!"

Would'st thou dwell in a forest home,
Where the giant cataract's ceaseless foam
Falls in showers of diamond dew,
Like hoary mists on the mountain blue;
While its jewelled crest of mimic bows,
Like flowery wreath in the sunbeam glows;
Where the Lascar, with his cane-oar, glides,
Like a winged thing, o'er their ocean tides;
Where the gloomy boughs of the cypress wave
In the deep ravine, o'er the red man's grave;
And many a flowery, green recess
Begems that leafy wilderness—
O'er prairies green, or savannahs fair,
Thou could'st wander free?—"Not there! not there!"

Would'st thou dwell where marble fanes
"Are veiled with wreaths on Italian plains,"
Where the myrtle, olive, and clustering vine,
On broken urn and fallen shrine,
Triumphal arch, with sculpture grey,
Hang nature's emerald drapery?
Where many a gorgeous palace towers,
By classic stream, 'mid orange bowers;
And the music-flow of leaping rills
Are singing low 'mong the vine-clad hills;
Where the rocks of that Eden clime have rung
To strains that Tasso and Petrarch sung,
And genius graves her marbles fair
With starry names?—"Not there! not there!"

Would'st dwell 'mid isles where the tropic-sun
Burns goldenly on the mountain's dun;
Where the tufted palm in beauty spreads
A fan-leaf crown on their lofty heads;
And the burnished wave, on "the coral strand,"
Washes the gold commingled sand;
Where the pearl-diver's evening song
Holds concert with the silver tone,
Stealing with low, mellifluous swell,
From the rosy lip of the music shell,
In hymn-like sound, so plaintive heard,
When wandering winds have gently stirred
The chords of Æolian harps, that play
Wild nature's untaught melody.

I love the mountains wildly grand—
The sea-girt isles of my fatherland—
Where the eagle wheels, and the cataract roars,
And tempests play on its rugged shores—
Where the thistle blooms, and the azure bell,
By the dark blue lake, on the heathy fell—
Where the song of the woods is "melodious and loud,"
And the martyr sleeps in his mossy shroud—
Where the rose blooms fair on the sylvan dells,
Cheered by the music of Sabbath bells;
Earth's Lyceum, where gigantic mind
Our souls with spells of beauty bind—
'Tis there I'd dwell, if you ask me where!
The graves, the homes of the loved are there.

What boots it whether we make our home
In the ivied cot or the pillared dome;
The rosy vale or the mountain wild;
The cloud-land or the sunshine mild;
'Mid arctic snows or "palm-flecked sands,"
Or the spicy groves of vernal lands?
Oh! the home of the heart is a home to me,
A land, a shrine, a sanctuary!
The thrilling touch of the clasping hand,
The smile of affection soft and bland,
The gentle tones of the gentle voice,
That make the drooping heart rejoice,
And the burning ray of the soul-lit eye,
When flashing with fervent poesy!

Let thy song be the eagle's, when soaring high—
"I was born on the earth, but I live in the sky;"
A warrior-bird, with tireless wing,
Up, up through the tempest journeying;
The world's zaara, a sandy wreath,
Its clouds and colds behind, beneath,
The inner eye upturned, away
From the mists of time to the God of day,
Drinking the light of the golden throne,
Where the waters of life flow on, still on,
Till the soul is bathed in the deep excess
Of the warmth and beauty of holiness;
When earth, on the pilgrim's eye, grows dark,
The bosom of God is the Home of the Heart.

O! I would dwell in a sinless sphere!
"We have no abiding city here."
'T is a land of crime—a land of graves—
Where the wasting storm of passion raves.
Where time revels o'er its bloom, and decay
Writes on its beauty—"passing away,"
Where the strains that hope the syren sings—
The smiles that joy from her sunshine flings—
The flowers around our path that spring,
Though fair, are brief and withering.
Where falsehood or death to coldness turns
The fervent love in the heart that burns,
And tears and darkness mantle all
The varying lights that around us fall.

There is a holy rest above—
A land of peace, of joy, and love;
No lips there are sealed in the hush of the tomb;
No worms revel over the rose's bloom;
No quivering lips, no pale cheeks tell
The agonies of a dark farewell!
Nor bleeding hearts in silence grieve,
That trusted ones of the soul deceive;
No dark thoughts cloud the brow with care;
Nor sin, nor sorrow, nor death is there;
No shadows fall on the eveless day,
Where the blaze of the throne shines eternally!
O ye who the ills of earth endure,
"Press on to the Rest, for the Home is sure!"

LAYS OF THE HEARTH.

"The 'fireside' is a seminary of infinite importance, because universal, and because the education it bestows being woven in with the woof of childhood, gives form and colour to the whole texture of life. There are few who can receive the honours of a college, but *all* are graduates of 'The Hearth.'"

LAYS OF THE HEARTH.

THE FIRST FLOWER.

NURSLING of the winter storm,
  Cradled in an icy bed,
Rearing fair thy fragile form,
  Drooping low thy humble head;
Herald of the dawning spring,
  First fruit of the budding flowers—
Peering from thy pillow green,
  'Mid our leafless bowers.

Prophecy of coming bloom,
  Augury of innumerous dyes—
Offering cups of rich perfume
  To the golden skies;
Opening verdure spreads her wing,
  Brooding o'er the budding earth—
Nursing germs of embryo spring
  Into beauteous birth!

Bursting from their shell-like tomb,
  As the chrysalis unfold
Iris wings of purple plume,
  Or enamelled gold;
Springing from their shroud of clay—
  From corruption dark and deep,
As the body from decay,
  And death's icy sleep.

In the crucible of earth
  Sunshine warms her frozen veins,
Waking to prolific birth
  Spring's unnumbered grains;
Garners, with exuberant breath,
  Winter's harvest of decay—
Fans the seeds of cradled death
  To garland golden day.

Mystic fancy! yet methinks,
  Bending to the throne of day,
Thus while life and light it drinks
  From the day-king's ray,
It emblems meet—a spotless one—
  Bathed in glory, robed in white,
Bending to the Ruler's throne—
  Beatified in light!

What is like thee—spotless bloom?
  Innocence is most like thee;
Purest 'mid affliction's gloom—
  Heaven-born humility!
Orisons, pure Mentor, raise
  High above earth's darkling strife,
Open up our hearts in praise
  To the Fount of Life.

May we cultivate with care,
  In its pure simplicity,
That lowly flower—so rich and rare-
  That angel grace, humility;
Thus the tiniest, simplest flower,
  Can Nature's mystic problems solve—
And in weakness, showing power,
  Mighty principles evolve.

Yea, the humblest blades of grass
  Teach the flower of life must die,
How our seasons come and pass,
  Swift as birds of travel fly;
Bearing o'er life's troubled wave,
  Precious seed, whose bud may be
On green lands—beyond the grave—
  Blossoms through Eternity!

SUMMER EMBLEMS.

"Sunshine and summer now with flowers
Light up the laughing earth."

THE young bud in the bloom,
And the blossom on the tree—
The breathing of perfume,
And the singing of the bee—
The flowers that deck the earth—
The music of the bowers—
The waters, singing mirth,
Proclaim the summer hours.
The shining, murmuring floods,
With the finny tribe are rife—
The greenery of woods,
With the hum of insect life—
The lamb on "flowery lea,"
Freed from the mountain-fold,
Disports, in buoyant glee,
O'er fields of green and gold.

The schoolboy seeks the brook
  To gambol in the tide,
Or cull in sunny nook
  The wild flowers on its side;
This golden summer noon,
  In sunshine smiling bright,
Flings o'er the blue of June
  A veil of silver light.
The water of the lakes
  Lies calm in stainless rest,
And scarce a ripple breaks
  The slumber of its breast;
And o'er that mimic sky
  No cloudy shadows pass,
But shining pictures lie
  Beneath, like painted glass.
The generating power
  Of the elements that feed
Is nursing into flower
  And fruit the bursting seed;
Is nourishing the vine
  On the sunny mountain-side,
"Where founts of purple wine"
  In luscious clusters hide.
And colouring the fruits
  That hold nectarious dew,
And bursting grain that shoots
  From the stem, with mellow hue,
Till earth, for Autumn's feast,
  Like a banquet-board is spread,

Whence man, and bird, and beast,
  Are liberally fed.
Oh ! praise the bounteous Power
  That earth with beauty fills;
And, like dew upon the flower,
  His silent gifts distils;
In gladness lift the voice,
  And the God of nature praise—
With thankful heart rejoice,
  For good are all his ways.

THE GENIUS OF SPRING.

"To cause the bud of the tender herb to spring forth.'

The nursling spring—like a dancing child,
With smiles on her opening lip so mild—
Comes decked with garlands of budding flowers,
Leading the glowing, golden hours.
Her tasseled vest, all gemmed with dew,
While promise breathes in her eye of blue;
And she gathers many a rich bouquet
From the budding boughs of the flowering tree,
And gaily flings, in her sunny mirth,
O'er these vernal children of the earth,
Fertile wreaths of the regal rose,
And "blossom-showers," like the cistus snows.
Her growing charms rich hues assume,
When summer unfolds her deep perfume,—
And the glorious sun can no shadow trace
On the cloudless light of her rosy face,
But violet-tufts, where her smiles have been,
Spangle the copses and meadows green;

Where sylvan streams come rippling by,
And groves are mirthful with melody,
And the carol of birds, in " choral swell,"
Ring jocundly in the sylvan dell.
All ye that hear the glad " voice of Spring,"
And think what stores her beauties bring,
And hope what her bloom fulfilled may be;
O! swell the anthem, and bend the knee,
Let meek devotion bend the head,
And thank the Lord for your daily bread.

SUMMER TWILIGHT.

"This holy hour is quiet as a nun
Breathless with adoration."

WORDSWORTH.

How sweet the summer twilight hours!
This Sabbath calm;
The breeze, now kissing closing flowers,
Is bland with balm;
The dews that whisper 'mid the leaves;
The folding rose;
Doth promise to the soul that grieves
A brief repose;
The birds have sung their vesper sóng
To dying day,
The "choral anthem's" latest tone
Has died away.
Behold yon pale and pensive star,
Herald of night!
Gemming the blue of heaven afar
With diamond light.
How sweet the soul-entrancing power
Of twilight's ray;
'T is adoration's breathing hour—
O, kneel and pray!

O! lift the heart up with the eyes,
Up, up to heaven;
The thoughts that in the breast arise
To God be given;
And pray that He our friends may guide
At last above;
And that while here, they still abide
In peace and love.
That when in death's dark, chilly night,
Their days decline,
Their souls in purer, higher light,
As stars may shine;
That heavenly hope to troubled breasts,
Toil-worn and riven,
May breathe the pledge of holy rest,
The peace of heaven!

THE FA' O' THE LEAF.

'TIS the fa' o' the leaf, and the cauld winds are blawin',
The wee birds, a' sangless, are dowie and wae;
The green leaf is sear, an' the brown leaf is fa'in,
Wan Nature lamentin' o'er simmer's decay.

Noo drumlie an' dark row the siller-like waters;
No a gowden-e'ed gowan on a' the green lea;
Her snell breath, wi' anger, in darkness noo scatters
The wee flowers, that danced to the sang o' the bee.

The green leaves o' simmer sing hopefu' an' cheerie,
When bonnie they smile in the sun's gowden ray;
But dowie, when sear leaves, in autumn winds eerie,
Sigh—"Life, love, and beauty, as flowers ye decay."

How waefu' the heart, where young hopes that gather,
Like spring-flowers in simmer, "are a' wede awa';"
An' the rose-bloom o' beauty, e'er autumn winds wither,
Like green leaves unfaded, lie cauld in the snaw.

But waefu' to see, as a naked tree lanely,
Man shake like a wan-leaf in poortith's cauld blast;
The last o' his kin, sighin', "Autumn is gane by,"
An' the wrinkles o' eild tell "his simmer is past."

The fire that 's blawn out, ance mair may be lighted,
An' a wee spark o' hope in the cauld heart may burn;
An' the "morning star" break on the travel-benighted,
An' day, wi' its fresh gushin' glories, return;

But dool, dool the fa', when shakes the clay sheilin',
An' the last keek o' day sets for ever in night!
When no ae wee star through the dark clud is stealin'
Thro' the cauld wave o' death, his dark spirit to light.

The spring-flowers o' life, a' sae blythsome and bonnie,
Though withered an' torn frae the heart far awa',
An' the flower we thocht fadeless—the fairest o' ony—
May spring up again whar nae freezin' winds blaw.

Kin' spring 'll woo back the green "bud to the timmer,"
Its heart burst in blossom 'neath simmer's warm breath
But when shall the warm blush o' life's faded simmer,
Bring back the rose-bloom frae the winter o' death?

How kin' should the heart be, aye warm an' forgi'en,
When sune, like a leaf, we maun a' fade awa';
When life's winter day as a shadow is fleein';
But simmer aye shines whar nae autumn leaves fa'!

OUR EARLY DAYS.

"Our childhood's cot we ne'er forget,
Though there we are forgot."

OUR early days! our early days!
Like silver lakes they lie,
Sun-pictured 'neath the golden rays
Of morning's cloudless sky:
Clear, in the distant vale of years,
Through memory's mist they shine,
Unruffled with the stormy tears
That dim life's after time.
Our early days—like streams they flow
Along our pilgrim-way,
Though shadowy hopes of "long ago,"
Like waters pass away;
But darkly in their channels deep,
The springs that filled them first,
O'er broken reeds may songless sweep,
And blight the flowers they nursed.
O! then, like pictures in a dream,
Sprung life's unfolding hours,
In April spring-light fresh and green,
Like fadeless, thornless flowers;

Those golden hours of careless youth
No shadows darkened then,
And earth was filled with spotless truth,
And happy, sinless men;
The skies then wore a brighter blue,
The earth a brighter bloom,
The spreading flowers that o'er it grew,
Hid deep the distant tomb.
And when, with wonder-stricken ear,
We gathered round the hearth,
Its tales of wild romance to hear,
And hushed our childhood's mirth;
The heart leapt up to join the dance
Of joy's delusive throng,
Where, 'neath the vale of beauty's trance,
Slept passions deep and strong;
That changed the wishing-cap we wore,
Its golden fruit we sought,
To ashes by the dead sea-shore,
All bitterness and drought.
O! many a rugged steep may lie
The sunny land between,
Where fancy wooes the sleepless eye
With everlasting green;
And rough and weary be the way
To glory's meteor star—
Like golden crowns that shine as day
On mountain-tops afar;
And youth may chase, from tree to tree,
The fabled bird of song,

That lures his steps o'er earth and sea,
'Mid fancy's rainbow throng;
And run through life's long summer hours,
To catch the flying joy,
And sleep at eve, 'mid faded flowers,
Calm as the Grecian boy;
While far around his early home,
With weary steps between,
In light that first around him shone,
Lie spots of brightest green.
O! never o'er earth's waste of wo,
He finds a calmer spot;
Or flowers of sweeter fragrance grow,
As round that ivied cot.
The homes—the hearths—are ne'er forgot,
Where childhood's love is set;
The very trees, whose shade we sought,
Are green on memory yet;
The voices that we loved to hear,
Each sweet, familiar tone,
Come rushing back on memory's ear,
And mingle with our own.
Our early friends—our early loved—
Come crowding through the brain;
Though cold in death, or far removed,
We wish them back again.
Upon each face, in memory's glass,
Back, back through tears we gaze,
Till warm upon our spirits pass
The *smiles of* early days.

The valleys, where we gathered flowers,
  Where, hand in hand we strayed,
When wand'ring the long summer hours,
  By hill, and stream, and glade;
Again, their thrilling hand we press;
  Again, we hear them speak;
Again, we lean upon their breast;
  Then wake in thought to weep;
Or wander to their grassy bed,
  And tread the paths they trod,
And hope, though lowly lies the head,
  Their spirit rests with God.
To drink the wave, still fresh and pure,
  From youth's untroubled spring,
Unmingled with the bitter lure
  Life's after-wand'rings bring;
But never shall we taste again
  The bounding, gushing glow
Of waters, which our spirit's pain
  We bathed in "long ago."
The streams that tell their place of birth,
  May seek their former track;
But life-waves wandering o'er the earth,
  O! never wander back!

TELL ME, GIRL, WHAT AILETH THEE?

"Why is your cheek so pale,—
How chance the roses that they fade so fast."

THE dance hath passed from thy spirit's glee,
Nor song is loud as it wont to be;
Silence shadows thy lip and eye,
Hushing the tone of its melody.
A smile hath passed from thy features fair,
Tears have dropped on thy shining hair,
Thought sits pale on thy lofty brow,
Fain would I read its vision now:
A captive sigh from thy spirit steals,
With fettered thought the lip conceals,
Where it trembles out from its hidden cell,
Faltering the grief it cannot tell.
Open the leaves of thy heart to me—
Tell me, girl, what aileth thee?

Is it the blight a false hope leaves?
When grief hath shaken her budding leaves—
Swept by the blast or the tempest-breath,
Thy flowers all laid in the dews of death,

Mourning the ashes of earthly trust,
'Graving, in marble—"dust to dust."
The thirst, when the pleasure-foam is quaffed;
The broken cup, and the scattered draught;
The spirit-burnings, that inly glow
With griefs the world may not know;
The broken shell, and its echoing tone,
When the lights are dead, and the dancers gone,
Gnawing thy heart, in its festal glee,
Asking thy spirit—"What aileth thee?"

Is the sunny wave of early song
Passing away, with its silver foam,
Falling in spray, on the rocks of time,
Like incense poured on a marble shrine?
The broken plume, and its dancing crest,
Like snow-fall melting on ocean's breast,
Ebbing away to the boundless deep,
Where the wrecks of time in darkness sleep—
Leaving the golden sands of life,
Furrowed with tears of its ocean-strife—
Strewing the shells of its silver sea
On the green, green rocks of memory.
The barque—is it far you ne'er may see?
Tell me, girl, what aileth thee?

Is thy yearning soul looking back, through tears,
"O'er the fields of fight in thy vanished years?"
Where sorrow walks 'mong its heaps of slain—
Turns o'er and o'er its dead again—

Looks on the faces, one by one,
Of the fallen joys where thy bosom clung,
But finds thy wishes cold and dead—
Pierced with the wounds its war hath made.
Say, hast thou leant on a broken reed?
Has it pierced thy heart till it inly bleed—
Breathing no tone of its river-lay,
Though swept by the breezes of Araby?
Ah! thou hast drank from the sateless streams—
That flow in song through this land of dreams—
The Marah-tide that from Eden, springs
Through the heart and its vain imaginings;
The poison-fruit of earth's Upas tree;
I know—now I know what aileth thee.

THE PARTING RAY.

"I knew by the paleness that came o'er her cheek,
And the hectic flush augured an early decay;
The tones of her voice grew so low and so weak—
The bloom of existence was passing away."

LIKE a fading ray, the hectic glow
Was dying on her cheek;
I saw her life's blood ebb and flow,
And heard her breathing deep.
Like starlight through a cloud, a ray
Came from her sunken eye,
As if her thoughts were wandering
'Mid "the glories of the sky:"
For, like a lessening ray of light,
Her lamp was on the wane;
Just lingering on the shades of night
To burst—to blaze again.
She spoke—her words were faint and few,
So like the trembling tone
That quivers on a broken harp—
Its mystic beauty gone.

The mortal turmoil in her breast
  Was troubled as the sea;
Her spirit, like a captured bird,
  Was fluttering to be free.
Low as the dreamings of a child,
  The whisperings of love,
Rose, murmuring from her spirit mild,
  In prayer to God above.
We watched her cheek grow pale and chill,
  We heard a broken sigh;
Her spirit passed so peacefully,
  We knew 't was bliss to die.
" The snowy garniture of death"
  Was braided o'er her brow;
They wrapt her in the sable shroud,
  And she is sleeping now.

'T IS AWAY, AWAY LIKE A STAR.

ON HEARING MISS A. M. P. LEE SAY, ON SEEING A BALLOON ASCENDING AT NIGHT, "ITS AWAY, AWAY LIKE A STAR."

"It died in beauty like a star,
Lost on the brow of day."

"AWAY, away like a star,"
Through the jewelled clouds of night,
As the "fire-fly lamp," through the ether far,
Arose that spirit-light.
Up, up as on eagle's wing,
A bark on a shoreless sea,
Like radiant thoughts, fast journeying
Through heaven's immensity.

Like bubbles children blow,
To silver bells in air,
That mount and shine in the iris glow,
As hopes that young hearts bear;
A vapour in their birth,
They fade on the aching eye,
A summer insect born of earth,
They breathe, they dance, and die.

A breath-stain upon glass,
  Too brief—to linger yet—
Our morning fancies featly pass,
  "They rise, they burn, they set."
Like rocket-stars to rise,
  Away in light to burn,
Till, lost 'mid the isles of the upper skies,
  Our spirits ne'er return.

Thus may we soar away,
  When earthly cords are riven,
Like an eagle bound for the eye of day,
  And lose ourselves in heaven.

A BRIDAL SONG.

TO —— —— ON HER MARRIAGE DAY.

Thou goest to another home,
  To wear another name,
To bear, through life, a human lot,
  Of mingled joy and pain;
And Time doth wave, o'er every way,
  A dark and silver wing,
And sun, and shadow, mark our day
  With joy and sorrowing.
Nor can I wish thy happy lot
  Untouched with tender tears,
For then it would not bear the hue
  Of any earthly years.
"O! love and life are mysteries,
  Both blessing and both blest—
Yet oft full much they teach the heart
  Of trial and unrest."

Though love has culled, with gentlest hand,
  The flowers that may not fade,
The fruits that in the future lie,
  Sleep in an untried shade;

Though hope now crowns, with golden light,
  Her mountain-tops of green,
In distance many a trial-step
  And steep may lie between.
The foam-bell on the sunny wave,
  O'er rocks, in song may flow,
While pearls, 'neath the darkest tide,
  In beauty sleep below;
Still, on the changing wheel of time,
  There moves an amber light—
A hand to trim the lamp of love –
  A star in every night.

Thy "loved one" to the altar leads
  Thee as his chosen bride,
And vows, before his God, to be
  Thy friend, thy guard, thy guide;
"Thy joy in grief—thy oracle"—
  Thy rest in sun and shade—
Companion through the vale of life—
  Thy husband, and thy head;
With whom thy inmost thought to share,
  Thy every hope to blend,
Thy love, thy comfort, and thy care—
  An ever-present friend,
Into whose sympathetic breast
  You safely may impart,
The very wants and weaknesses—
  The *tremblings* of thy heart.

Protector of the fatherless!—
O! may He ever be,
A shield, a counsel, a delight,
A glory unto thee!
And thou shalt be the cheering light
That warms his evening hearth,
To brighten, with thy beaming smiles,
Long hours of joy and mirth;
With more than even a father's love—
More than a mother's care,
May he—a jewel on his heart—
Thy worth and goodness wear;
And friends, who on this joyous day,
See mingled hearts sealed one,
Shall watch the silver stream of love
To death's dark river run.

While peace shall gild its sunny wave,
Your praise shall be its song—
"Their heads are crowned with silver age,
But still their hearts are young;"
May all that in the golden ring
Of plighted love can blend,
And all that human love can bring,
Still circle thee, my friend;
May all that crowns an earthly wish,
And brims the cup of joy,
Long mingle in the sacred bonds
That Time may not destroy;

All, all that in the happy home
  Of wedded spirits shine,
And showers of blessing, from above,
  Be poured "on thee and thine."

LINES ADDRESSED TO ——

I 'VE twined a bright, a lovely flower,
With this poetic dream,
And pardon me if thou shouldst be
The spirit of my theme;
The winning charm of gracefulness
Has flung its spell o'er me,
And links my soul, by tender ties
Of gentleness, to thee.
There are of souls so formed to please,
We hail at first as friends,
Nor wait till time, by slow degrees,
" Our hearts and feelings blends."
And now, methinks, I gaze upon
Thy sweet expressive face,
And there a tale of glowing thought,
In radiant lines I trace.
Thy features sweetly eloquent—
Thy lofty marble brow,
Each soul-expressive lineament
Is breathing beauty now;
These bear upon their every hue
The impress of a mind,

The fount of many a glowing thought
By genius, taste, refined;
And like the starry gems inert,
In far Golconda's mine,
The hidden treasures of thy soul
Like burning diamonds shine;
I 've felt the intellectual gleam
Of feeling pure and high,
That radiates in the thrilling beam
Of thine expressive eye;
I would that sorrow's weary touch
May never stain with gloom,
The eye of blue, of azure blue,
The sunny blue of June;
I would the burning tear of grief
May never, never tinge
That eye, "save pity drop relief"
From off its silken fringe;
But love has thrown a pensiveness
Upon that virgin-brow,
For surely sorrow cannot dim
Its sunny beauty now?
And, ah! methinks I read upon
Thy lips so bland and sweet,
The signet of a spirit fraught
With love intensely deep—
The roseate blush, the downcast eye,
All silently reveal
The deep unuttered tenderness,
Thy spirit would conceal.

If thou wilt give the name of friend
 To such an one as me,
The fondest feelings of my soul
 I 'd freely proffer thee;
For, oh! I love a kindred soul,
 A warm congenial heart,
To whom I might, with confidence,
 A secret thought impart,
To blend our spirits melted flow,
 Like two congenial streams;
Commingle thoughts ecstatic glow
 In poesy's flowery dreams.
And in the fervid orison,
 Where fondest wishes blend,
I 'll plead for heaven's benison
 To guide and guard my friend;
To lead thee o'er a thornless plain,
 A flower-enamelled way,
That life may be a dream of love,
 A long, long summer day—
To lead thee through the vale of death,
 The portals of the tomb,
To yonder glory-gilded home,
 Where flowers perennial bloom.

TO MY FRIEND, JESSIE, ON HER BIRTHDAY.

—"Who has not felt how dear are all those tender sympathies that link the soul in gentleness together?"

THY name has still a power like music o'er me,
  The same high power it held in other days;
Thy face still smiles in loveliness before me,
  Lit with the sunshine of thy mind's soft rays;
Thy smile has still the same alluring spell;
  Thy voice wears still affection's blandest tone,
Stirring my bosom with a burning swell,
  Like the rich melody of some old song.
The same dark ringlet that you loved to wear,
  I memoried oft in pencilings of thee;
Those tresses, dark as night, of silken hair,
  That curled on thy cheek so gracefully.
I feel the beamings of thy fine blue eye,
  Its soul-o'erweening and magnetic power,
Unlocking treasure-sympathies, that lie
  In the rich depths of thought's uncounted dower.

I feel the thrillings of our early feelings,
The flush of joy that in the young heart springs,
That coloured all our mingled heart-revealings,
With the rich hues of hope's imaginings;
When wreathing in the rose-enwoven bowers
Of song and flowers, most delicate bouquets;
And morn was redolent of opening flowers,
And hope drew pictures every wish to please;
Yet now, methinks, a paler caste of thought,
A calmer tone of dignity I trace,
Though nothing less of beauty—love has wrought
On the deep eloquence of thy sweet face.
And thou art still in beauty's opening flower,
Thy fervent feelings in their morning spring:
Thy sunny youth is in its regal power,
Yea, not a grace is chilled and withering.
But thou hast felt the trials of the heart,
Which all must struggle with, and all must bear,
That fling a shadow o'er life's brightest part,
Those little griefs to which our race is heir.
The heir-loom that our sin-born heart bequeaths,
That wean the soul from passing gauds of earth,
And close, and closer, round our nature wreath
The soul-enduring bonds of heavenly birth.
When the rose-hues of summer autumn sears,
These leaves of evergreen shall cling and twine,
'Mid the far shadows of our early years,
Round the grey ruin of life's after-time.
And may you ever have, in hours of sadness,
Fond friendship's faithful arm whereon to rest;

Love's soothing hand, to pour the oil of gladness
  In every wound that aches within your breast.
I would not have the ills that chill the crowd
  Shadow thy day with storms of sorrow's night,
But pass, as over flowers the summer cloud,
  That makes their beauty grow in tears more bright.
One wish shall ever with my prayer blend,
  One hope, where'er our distant way may be,
That I before the Throne of Love may spend
  A long eternity of praise with thee.

THE FATHERLESS.

"What though no anxious hand may fill
For them life's flowing cup;
Though earth and kindred all forsake,
'The Lord will take them up.'"

THE orphan and the fatherless
"Are God's peculiar care;"
Let them your tender sympathy
And loving-kindness share.
Though tempests sweep life's olive-flowers,
And cut the parent stem,
There hangeth on the stranger bough
Still gleaning grapes for them.
O! who would chide the fatherless,
Or make the orphan weep,
When strangers by the bed of pain
Must watch their troubled sleep;
A sister's love, a brother's care:—
Yes, these are sacred things;
But streams have not the constant flow
With which the fountain springs.
To-day, the rains that swell their bed,
To-morrow's sun may dry;

And human hearts, like mountain brooks,
Oft deal deceitfully.
Who so supplies those little wants,
By which "this clay thing" lives—
The wants a mother only knows,
Unasked, a father gives.
A "Father," named in careless tone,
The orphan heart may swell,
With pangs that silence breathes alone,
The tongue may never tell.
All fresh as Pompeii's buried stores,
Though long, long years have fled,
The lava of the burning heart
Restores their cherished dead;
The old arm chair—the Bible old—
The board—the evening fire;
Each old familiar thing he loved,
Recall the absent sire;
The very pictures on the wall,
The songs he loved to hear,
Embalm, in living tone and hue,
The form to memory dear.
That first great grief, whose bursting flood,
Their roof-tree bore away;
That wildering sense of loneliness,
That clasped the cold, cold clay;
The sable crowd—the faces pale—
The closed and darkened room—
The voices low—the murky dress—
The winding-sheet—the tomb.

They seek or shun the old green paths,
Marked by a father's tread;
His spirit lingers 'mid the trees,
And whispers in the shade.
Who would not love the fatherless?
The thought—the very name,
O'erfills our hearts with tenderness,
And love almost like pain.
Ah! who would dare the frown of heaven,
The Meroz curse to brave,
By wounding hearts, whose shielding arm
Lies powerless in the grave!

"CHILDHOOD'S PRAYER."

> "Child, amid the flowers at play,
> While the red light fades away,
> Pray, ere yet the dark hours be,
> Lift the heart and bend the knee."

O! Is there aught so pure on earth
As childhood's holy lisping prayer?
When holy thoughts have hushed the mirth
Their bounding bird-like spirits bear.

When closed, so meek, the radiant eye,
The sunny gambols' careless glee;
The fair young brow, so solemnly,
Bent calmly by the fostering knee.

When the young heart is taught to rise,
And plead for "angel-guards" in sleep,
And ask "Our Father," in the skies,
Their friends and kindred dear to keep.

To think *that* lowly silver tone
Is heard 'mid angel-harps on high,
And charms, as meet as seraph's song,
The ear of list'ning Deity.

A rose-bud, swayed by smiles and tears,
And changeable as wild dove's wing,
Is childhood—ere the world sears
The heart with blight or sorrowing.

A holy trust—to mortals given,
To nurture blossoms for the sky;
To train for Eden-fruits in heaven,
Those germs of immortality.

Lambs of the heavenly fold—O! feed
On "pastures green" the gentle flock;
Them, by the living way, oh! lead
To Him who says, "Forbid them not."

I think of Him—to see a child
To gentle bosoms fondly pressed,
Who, in his arms, with accents mild,
Such little children kindly blest.

The infant mind, as wax, will take
Impressions of the finest mould;
But Satan draws, in many a shape,
His image on the tarnished gold.

Watch—pray—that the Refiner sit
And purge it, till His image shines
In perfect stature, rendered fit
To glow in light that ne'er declines.

THE HERD LADDIE.

A HERD laddie sat, in his plaidie o'grey,
'Neath the beild o' a bush in the howe o' a brae,
On the moss-theekit stump o' an auld aiken tree,
By a wee wimplin' burnie that sang to the sea,
And silvered the hem o' a bonnie green knowe,
Whar the broom-bush, and breckan, and primroses grow:
As wee stars that glimmer like sprinklins o' gowd,
As they blink through the blue o' the grey e'ening cloud,
His sheep lay besprent on the green mountain's breast,
As white as the snaw-cleeded gowan they prest—
Where the lammies were bleatin', an' jumpin' wi' glee,
An' nibblin' the gowan that spangled the lea;
Noo laughin' an' dancin' like youth's mornin' wave,
Ere it wanders an' yaummers awa' to the grave.
The herd laddie doffed his wee bonnet, an' smiled,
But a tear in his dark ee my heart near him wyled,
Like an amber-bead trickled adown his brown cheek,
Clear as pearlins o' dew-draps that glanced at his feet:
I said, "Wee herd laddie, what maks you sae wae,
A' nature around you is smilin' an' gay—

Come, tell me your story, I'll sit by your side—
What book 's that your hidin' aneath the grey plaid ?
Are ye cauld, are ye hungry? is 't far frae your hame ?
Hae ye faither or mither ?" He sighed—"I hae nane.
Yon bonnie cot house in the lap o' the glen,
When a bairnie, I toddled its but an' its ben;
When I leuk till 't I greet—for that ance was my hame—
Noo faither, and mither, an' help I hae nane;
Syne the nicht faither dee't gushes back to my mind,
Though maister an' mistress to me are fu' kind;
An' there is the psalm round his bed that we sung—
I hear his last words drappin' yet frae his tongue:
O, the tears happit fast frae his dim closin' e'e !
When he blest us, an' tauld us his bairns he maun lea'e;
An' that is his Bible he gied me, an' said,
'Mind your Father in heaven, my bairns, when I'm dead;'
When my wee brithers grat round the auld elbow chair—
For he learned us the psalms on the Sabbath e'en there;
And we kneeled on that hearth-stane whar uncos noo meet;
When I think I've nae hame, oh ! what wonder I greet;
But I leuk to the skies, an' I ken there is ane
Wha lo'es me an' guides me, tho' on earth I hae nane."

Oh! the heart that ne'er warms for the faitherless bairn
Is hard as the millstane, an' cauld as the airn;
Oh ! daut them and cleed them, wi' mitherly care—
They are nurslings o' heaven—oh ! nurse them wi' prayer.

THE RUINED COT.

"All! all—alas! are gone—
Scattered and parted far and near,
Who in one circle shone."

LOST ONE.

IN the shadow of a mountain wood,
In a ruin mossy grey,
On a deserted hearth we stood,
To muse on life's decay:
The fox-glove in the lattice grew,
With spiral-tufted bells,
The wild bee honey treasures drew—
Pure from its purpled cells;
The ivy o'er the threshold crept,
Where gladdening steps had passed—
Where radiant eyes o'er partings wept,
And loved ones looked their last,—
Where home-sick wand'rers oft returned,
From stranger land, or main,—
Where beating hearts with joy once burned
To greet their home again,—
Where lost ones sought the loved they left,
When silence echoed—"where?"

And read the tale of hearts bereft,
 Writ on "a vacant chair."
The grasshopper chirped on the hearth,
 Where household voices sang
The evening psalm—and childhood's mirth
 In bird-like carols rang;
The thistle reared its loftly head,
 Where flowers of cherished bloom
Their beauty and deep fragrance spread,
 Now faded in the tomb.
The family band in thought I drew,
 That nightly gathered there,
When holy words, like evening dew,
 Bowed low the head in prayer;
The father with his hoary head
 Bent o'er the evening meal,
Begs blessings on the children's bread,
 And blessings for their weal;
The old arm chair they gather near,
 With looks and words of fun,
Where tales of eld they marv'lling hear,
 Day's sunny gambol run.
Now who may trace those springs of life,
 That Time's all-wrecking wave
Has parted far in ocean strife,
 And find each wanderer's grave?
Fair faces scattered—closed in night
 Bright eyes, whose joy and mirth
Circled, with smiles of love and light,
 The cold and darkened hearth;

Where boyhood, in its bounding joy,
  Dashed out its crystal wave,
As green earth for the careless boy
  Concealed no wasting grave.
The streams that from one fountain gush,
  Take many a devious way,
Some darkly to the ocean rush,
  Some clear in sunshine stray;
Some glide o'er many a flowery land,
  In beauty calm and deep;
Some roaring o'er a rocky strand,
  Their restless waters sweep.
And who that sees youth's silver stream,
  By no dark wand'rings tossed,
Can tell how far 'twill sigh or sing,
  Where sink its waters lost?

THE BROTHERS.

AN OLD LADY WEEPING OVER A PICTURE—HER DAUGH' WITH ANOTHER IN HER HAND, ASKING HER TO TELL STORY OF EACH.

"DEAR MOTHER, wipe your tears—they stain
That lovely pictured face;
I 'll hang it on the wall again,
In its familiar place.
Why weep, and wherefore gaze so long
On that pale shadowy brow?
When did my brothers leave our home;
Where are they wandering now?

"And this one has his father's eye,
His cheek a brighter glow;
But, when I ask his name, you sigh,
And whisper, 'long ago.'
That tinselled cloak—that lordly look—
That high patrician air—
Methinks his spirit ill could brook
What meeker natures bear."

"O! yes, he was a noble boy,
A rose-bloom, in his pride—
His brother, like a violet, grew
In meekness by his side;
And yet it seems but yesterday,
A sunbeam in his joy,
He bounded here, in dancing play—
That happy, careless boy.

"While oft I smoothed his golden hair,
And kissed his rosy cheek,
Spring's opening buds, in sunshine fair,
Smiled calm in hope's young sleep:
He oft, with step of martial pride,
Would plead his sire to tell
How warrior men, in glory, died,
How heroes fought and fell.

"He shouted the long summer day
The rocks and woods among,
And brought the wild fruit from the spray,
That o'er the cataract hung.
The fire that lit his falcon eye
Spake prophecies of doom,
Foretold the strife of destiny—
He wore the martial plume."

"And tell me, will he ne'er return
From stranger-land afar?
How did his fiery spirit burn
On the red field of war?"

"He comes no more to cheer our hearth,
No dream his memory fills
With echoes of his boyhood mirth,
Amid his own blue hills.

"No friend may weep where he is laid,
Or trace the wanderer's tale—
He sleeps beneath the palm tree's shade,
Far in an Indian vale.
And yet I like the milder grace
Of *this* dark lustrous eye;
For thought looks out from his meek face,
In feelings pure and high.

"His last fond look I'll ne'er forget—
To bless us with his smile,
He turned and lingered on that step,
And hid his tears the while.
Oft with pale brow and thoughtful look,
With meek and solemn air,
He, marvelling, conned the Holy Book,
The deep Love treasured there.

"A creature easily passed by,
Where rung his brother's glee,
Who joyed beneath his mother's eye,
And sat beside her knee;
And wept, and wondered, when she told
Of sainted martyr men,
From books familiar and old,
Whose grave-stones deck the glen.

"Who, for *that* Love, all homeless trod
  The wild, nor recked the strife—
Who, by faith, glorified their God,
  And trial sealed with life :
The spark, then smouldering in his heart,
  Burned out a living flame,
And shone a light to nations dark,
  In glory starred his name.

"He bore across the stormy wave,
  Like deluge-missioned dove,
The life-lamp to the prisoned slave,
  'The branch of peace and love.'
A green spot marks his place of rest,
  Where Indians bend the knee,
And plant fair flowers upon his breast,
  'Neath the Banana tree."

LOST ONES.

"When all, by death and fate removed,
Like spirits crowd upon the eye;
The few we liked—the one we loved—
And the whole heart is memory."

WHERE are the friends that bound us
By their spells in early hours,
And in beauty bloomed around us,
Like opening summer flowers?
Whose words of balmy pleasure,
Made a garden of the earth;
Our sweetest earth-born treasure,
Their smiles around the hearth?

Now, where are those we cherished,
In joyance and in pride,
Whose opening graces flourished
Into blossom by our side?
Ah! some are mingling with the clay,
Like sear autumnal leaves;
And others wafted far away,
Beyond the distant seas;

And some, amid the white sea-shells,
Are sleeping 'neath the wave—
The murmur of the billow swells
In dirges o'er their grave;

And many, fallen in their bloom,
  In beauty's early prime,
Now slumber in the silent tomb,
  Nor feel the lapse of time.

And others, dazzled by the sheen,
  The purple pomp of war,
Now chase the "ignis fatuus" gleam
  Of glory's changing star.
Some, guided by ambitious pride,
  To win a lauded name,
Are wrestling with the glittering tide,
  That lures to wealth or fame.

And those, whose soul-inspiring light
  Shed radiance o'er our way,
Arose, like meteors, on our sight,
  To burn and pass away.
The hopes we dreamt would ne'er decay
  Have brimmed our souls with grief,
And faded from our hearts away,
  Like flowerets, leaf by leaf.

The tenderest sympathies of life,
  That with our heart-strings twine,
Are severed by the jarring strife
  Of desolating time.
Then lay your treasure in the skies,
  Nor build on earth your trust,
For soon its morning glory lies
  In darkness, death, and dust!

THE EMIGRANT TO HIS FATHERLANI

RESPECTFULLY INSCRIBED TO J. B. BROWNE, ESQ., AU
"VIEWS OF CANADA AND THE COLONISTS."

WHAT marvel that I love thee,
Thou land of rock and rill;
My heart, 'mid pleasant memories,
Is dwelling with thee still!
What marvel that I love thee,
As a bridegroom loves his bride,
For methinks I'm in thy pleasant homes,
And seated by the side
Of friends, whose gentle voices
Still are ringing in my ear;
My heart beats with a warmer thrill
Their kindly tones to hear.
I see them still before me,
Each fair and lofty brow—
Their eyes, in melting tenderness,
Are beaming on me now.
I feel them stir my bosom,
Each smile and clasping hand—

The lip of rose, that frequent breathed
  Affection soft and bland.
I'm wand'ring through thy pleasant woods,
  And by thy deep blue lake,
Where leaping rills, in leafy glades,
  A pensive music make;
Where Autumn's rich and myriad dyes,
  And sunny shadows fell,
On rock, and isle, and ferny brake,
  Of my loved native dell;
Where sunset wove her gorgeous hues
  On ev'ning's purple crest,
And mirrored her fantastic shapes
  Upon the water's breast;
Where clouds of bronze and violet
  Their varied shadows flung,
And canopies, with golden fringe,
  In regal grandeur hung.
I'm gazing on thy weed-grown towers—
  The monuments of yore—
Whose fallen stones the legends tell
  Of ancient feudal lore.
I'm standing by the altar stones
  That crown the heathy fell,
Whose mossy cairns, of Druid rites
  And grey traditions tell.
I've hungered for the beautiful
  Since feeling's earliest hour—
A love of nature and its pomp
  Has been my richest dower;

I love the holy harpings
  Of the lyre's melodious strings—
My heart re-echoes every note
  Thy hoary minstrel sings.
O land of many temples!
  "O land of gifted men!"
My yearning heart is languishing
  To visit thee again.
What marvel that I love thee—
  Thy hills, thy streams, and dells!
What marvel that ye chain my soul
  In all your music spells!
Even as a weaned child unto
  Its mother's bosom clings,
Though seas have borne me far away,
  My spirit backward springs.

ABSENT VOICES.

"O! absence, with a yearning power,
My soul has ever stirred,
And trembled o'er the lingering hour
That haunts the parting word;
And strange fond moods the spirit hath,
That never tread life's common path."

Ye voices! O, ye voices
Of the absent and the dead!
Ye haunt my soul with melody,
Although your tones are fled;
Ye are floating like rose odours
On every passing breeze—
Like green leaves from the shaking bough,
Or music from the seas;
Ye rush across my heart-strings
With pathos rich and deep;
Ye sing in silence to my soul,
And murmur in my sleep.
Ye voices! absent voices!
Why mock me with your tone,
And stir my heart with memories
And dreams of beauty gone?

Return! ye "flute-like voices,"
With your bland and holy lays,
And waken, by the clasping hand,
Our spirit-harmonies.
Come with your strains of gladness—
All silent—answer me;
Have you no thoughts of sadness—
No song of early glee?
I languish for your music-notes,
Like harpings from above;
Your moanings low, and solitude,
As plaintive mourning dove.
Hope whispers ye will soon return
To still this yearning pain,
And pour, from friendship's golden urn,
The oil of joy again.
The memory of music gone—
A tale of faded bloom—
A cadence hushing in its tone—
A requiem o'er the tomb.
The fallen lights of other years,
Relumed by memory's power,
Their shadowy shapes of beauty throw
Around the lonely hour;
When the yearning fount of sympathy
Is brimmed to rich excess,
And we sicken 'neath intensity
Of thoughts we can't express;
Till, overful with sympathy,
The tear-cup overflows—

Till inly to the throbbing heart
  A whispered prayer glows.
No echoes from the slumbering dead!
  Are ye for ever mute?
What hand may waken music
  From a stringless, broken lute?
The wind sweeps o'er the shattered frame
  That silent, soulless lies,
But who may gather from the dust
  The spirit-melodies?
A flower, a look, a music note,
  A softly whispered word,
May rush in voices to the soul,
  And thrill its finest chord;
The burden of a voiceless thought,
  A tear in silence shed,
The prayer that craves a gift of light,
  Are echoes from the dead;
The bond that closer wreathes the ties
  That twine till we shall see
Commingled spirits, filled with love
  That fills eternity—
The peace that only one bestows
  Within our bosoms dwell,
The joy from living hope that flows,
  That breathes of no *farewell.*

"I SEEK A BRIGHTER LAND."

This title is the motto to a beautiful emblematic device on a representing sunset on the sea; a dove, with wings outspread, lea in the distance "the village church among the trees."

THE stars that light our nether heaven,
  Like sunshine on a wint'ry day;
Or clouds before the tempest driven,
  Shine on the heart and pass away.

While on a lovely face we gaze,
  Where radiates all the soul of feeling;
In thrilling tones the spirit-rays
  Die on the ear—in thought—revealing.

And should we meet a kindred heart
  Where gush affection's jewelled waters—
Time's iron tongue soon bids us part,
  Some rock our mingled feeling scatters.

The tear is gathering in the eye
  Still beaming with the soul's fond greeting,
In distance see our pathway lie
  Dissevered—while glad friends are meeting.

Even while we linger by the wells
  In shady spots 'mong spirit bands,
The longing, thirsting soul out-wells,
  In yearnings for yon brighter lands.

The brightest sun sets in the sea,
  The wave is ebbing while it flows;
The spirit longs for wings to flee,
  When evening "shuts in tears the rose."

Yet, there are holy spots on earth
  From which the bosom bleeds to part –
Dear as the island of our birth,
  And ever green upon our heart.

Remembrance hallows with her tear
  Our early hearth—our early home;
The very stones to us are dear,
  That echo back our childhood song.

The green, green spots where friends have met,
  The old church 'mid the old yew trees,
Whose song in echoes linger yet,
  Flung back on memory's wand'ring breeze.

We may not lean the weary breast
  By palmy oasis—e'er so green;
For pilgrims know 'tis not their rest,
  They seek a city—yet unseen.

Then tempt, O! tempt me not to say,
With gentle accents warm and bland;
O! Cut the leash, I must away—
I seek—I seek—a brighter land!

There you may pour, unchecked and free,
The heart's unchilled, unbroken glow;
Love, quenchless as the meteless sea,
Where none may chide its fountain-flow.

No sun, in shadow there declines,
No bird of travel spreads the wing,
No sea divides with parting lines,
The home-land of eternal spring.

Our life may not be all a dream
Of love; we may not pause and weep,
But still fight on, and only seem,
With tears and smiles, night-watch to keep.

When music lures thee with her song,
And joy would hold thy ling'ring hand,
And chain thee with "one golden tone,"—
Arise! and seek that brighter land!

THE DEPARTURE.

"I faint beneath a nobler wound nor love below the skies."

Low breathings filled a darkened room,
  The voice of sighing prayer,
Departing sunlight's dewy gloom;
The boding shadows of the tomb,
  Pale faces, gathered there.

And eyes, like dew-filled violets, bowed
  To catch the parting ray,
Watching the soul's dissolving shroud
To radiance, like a silver cloud,
  In glory melt away.

A pilgrim neared the goodly land,
  Beside the vale of shade;
His kindred press the chilly hand,
But fond farewells and voices bland,
  In airy distance fade.

Earth-shadows, in the vale of night,
Were dark'ning o'er his eyes;
The smiles, that fostered high delight,
Grew strange and dark in growing light,
And vanished in the skies.

His friend with face beloved came near
To seek the parting look,
Who, for his griefs, had still a tear;
Unknown the tones that once could cheer,
They not a heart-string shook.

He knoweth not his only-born,
His mother's hope and joy,
Whose spirit, on his own upborn,
He fanned to prayer, night and morn—
Unseen, his bright-eyed boy.

Nor she, pale watcher, by his bed,
Deep sorrow on her cheek,
Who flitted, with a whispered tread,
To smooth the pillow for his head
When earth was hushed in sleep.

Who bright, amid earth's stormy war,
A guiding beacon shone;
Who lured to joy while toiling far,
And rose, an ever-watchful star,
Like peace, above his home.

Nor he, the holy man of God,
  Who whispered in his ear
The name of One who held the rod
To guide the way he weary trod—
  That name wakes death's dull ear.

"I know Him, my Redeemer, well,"
  The sinking pilgrim cried;
"Nor earth, nor sin, nor death, nor hell,
Shall ever break the mystic spell
  That marks the *crucified*."

THE WATER LILY.

TO A. RITCHIE, ESQ.

"——-——Springing into light,
Still buoyantly above the billows' might,
Through the storm's breath ——."

Flower of the stately mien!
So sculpture-like in grace,
Lifting, above the wave, serene,
To heaven, thy placid face;
Born in the weltering wave,
And cradled on its breast,
The pure in heart, thus trembling, brave
Earth's dark and deep unrest;
And shine above life's troubled sea,
In heaven's reflected purity.

Thy head oft bent with tears—
Rich pearls in thy heart—
You smile in light, 'mid swelling fears,
And kiss the billows dark;

Thy life is in the wave,
  Thy bloom no tempests move;
Thus faith looks up from nature's grave,
  To Heaven's pure eye of love;
Deep-rooted in affliction's sea;
Calm in hope's immortality.

An altar and an ark,
  Thy snow-enamelled cup,
Offering to heaven, from thy pure heart,
  Thy soul's deep fragrance up;
Trembling on "life's dull stream,"
  Oft broken by the blast,
Still meekly brave where dangers teem—
  In floods established fast;
Though, reed-like, shaken by a breath,
You fearless brave the wave of death.

THE GIPSY.

ROMANCE has pictured thee with colours gay,
With rose-wreathed cap, and hair of falcon wing,
Creeping through woodlands like a summer's ray;
Dancing, or sleeping, by the forest stream;
Waking, with cuckoo song, the dusky dell;
Seeking, with wild-dove wing, the hunter's lair;
Alluring ignorance with prophet spell;
Haunting the violet-nooks when skies are fair.
Bland nature's child—"a weed of glorious feature"—
A sportive fawn—a free, a happy creature;
But truth has writ beneath that masque of dress,
"A child of darkness, swathed in wretchedness."

TWIN FLOWERS.

LINES ON TWO BROTHERS, WHO DIED SUDDENLY, ON 1ST DECEMBER, 1841, AND WERE BURIED ON ONE DAY.

"THEY sleep in beauty, side by side,"
In one cold shroud of clay;
Borne, in their childhood's budding pride,
On one dark bier away;
Torn from a father's fond caress,
A mother's watchful tenderness.

With brows like sculptured marble fair,
Their all, their only born;
So rose-like, with their golden hair,
As cradled dews of morn;
Swept by a sudden blast to earth;
A sun-ray in their life and birth.

The mother, by the silent hearth,
Broods o'er their little joys;
Hears, with her heart, their gleesome mirth,
And cries, "My boys! my boys!
My broken buds are fading now!
But sorrow cannot touch their brow!"

And oft she hears their dancing feet
  Upon the threshold play,
Who ran, with dance and song, to meet
  Their sire, when sunset lay
In crimson shadows on the stream—
Alas! tis memory's waking dream!

She hears them in the primrose glade;
  But, ah! that bird-like tone,
Those silvery echoes, where they played,
  Is but the cuckoo's song;
Their voice, e'en like its springtide lay,
Passing to brighter lands away.

And still she cradles them in dreams,
  Kissing each rosy cheek;
And still their blue eyes hide their beams,
  Upon her breast to weep;
But memory wakes, and seeks the spot,
That writes in dust—that they "are not!"

O! better thus in spring depart,
  To sing in brighter skies,
Than brook the with'ring of the heart,
  That weeps o'er severed ties;
Dark shadows tell, where sunbeams pass,
That life "is like the flower of grass."

And broken is each silvery string
  That binds to earthly love,
That we may clear the clouds, and sing
  In higher strains above;
The skylark never sings so loud
As when he cleaves the sunny cloud.

And they, in age, had wept, mayhap,
  Oft o'er the early dead;
Or pillowed on a stranger's lap,
  A sick and weary head;
And heard, in dreams of distant home,
An absent voice—a mother's song.

Or, they had pierced with many a thorn
  The doating parent's breast;
Or bowed the grey head, sorrow-worn,
  To an untimely rest;
Or sunk in sin 'mid woes that sear,
Unhallowed by repentant tear.

O'er weary tracts of sunless gloom,
  Had rolled life's troubled wave,
And sunk, where no spring flow'rets bloom,
  Dark in an ocean grave,—
A life-wreck, tossing o'er and o'er,
The restless wave that finds no shore.

Weep not for those whose tears are o'er,
  Like dew in morning's glow;
"They are not lost, but gone before,"
  To shine in mercy's bow:
And radiant may love's circle rise,
To burn unbroken—in the skies.

But weep for those whose golden bowl
  Is broken, not in dust;
Who drink the bitter waves that roll
  From earth's deceitful trust;
Who, in the waste of rain-drops, dream,
And, waking, see the mirage gleam.

And ne'er from broken cisterns seek
  Springs of unfailing birth,
Death o'er its fairest flow'rets sweep—
  O! seek them not on earth;
In lowliness, then, kiss the rod,
And seek unchanging joy in God!

ON A SPRIG OF IVY.

INSCRIBED TO
MISS AUGUSTA J—— H——, OF M—— H——.

THE clinging, clasping ivy,
  Its ever-vernal leaves
Around the oak and ruin
  A wreath of verdure weaves;
Its viewless life-roots twining,
  Green, o'er the blasted tree,
Above dark life-wrecks shining,
  Like woman's constancy.
When man's oak heart is shaken,
  And bowed his palmy crest,
By his parent earth forsaken,
  Still woman binds his breast;
With constant love still creeping
  Where his haughty head lies low;
When sorrow's blast is sweeping
  The bent and broken bough;
With *hope's* green wreath still shading,
  Decay with second Spring.
When the last green leaf is fading
  'Neath Autumn's searing wing,
She mantles up the *ruin*
  Of his cold and blighted heart,
By faith, to heaven wooing
  His being's better part.

THE STRANGER'S FUNERAL.

SKETCHES FROM LIFE IN CITY LANES, TAKEN ON THE SPOT. SCENE—A MOTLEY GROUP OF MEN, WOMEN, AND CHILDREN FOLLOWING A BIER, WITHOUT ONE MOURNER.

It would have pierced the iron of stoniest heart—
Melted its "granite" till it flowed in tears
Of sympathy, for the dumb corpse that lay,
And begged a burial from the passing crowd,
Like some foul offal which the dogs might bury,
Cast from the ragged lap of beggared want.
So crime-stained seemed the bier that had no mourner—
The last stay of the lonely motherless.
Clay of our kin—yet think how dear to her
Who wept unseen—no father, brother, near—
For friend to hear her "Mother," dead and cold,
Her last lone help, her friend, her home, her all.
Oh! had it been a city of the dead,
Where withering plagues had frozen every stream
Of warm humanity, the charnel cart
Had stopped, even here, and dragged it to the shade
Of unmarked graves, 'mong suicidal dead.
No solemn group came near in silken black,

To image forth a grief they did not feel;
The scarcely blackened boards
Together nailed by pnblic charity;
The nameless, palless, and uncovered lid,
Untinselled with the 'scutcheons of the tomb,
Was but a flouting of death's heraldry,
And merely aped the right of sepulture;
But there, from noon till shut of day, it begged
The common right of mere humanity—
A friendly hand to cover it with dust,
For 'twas a thing which poverty had cursed,
Which even pitying charity denied.
And sympathy had not a single tear
For the *coarse* clay the passer loathed to touch,
As a plague-spotted thing which none would own;
An Upas showering pestilential dews,
As all who breathed in sight of which would fever,
And all who touched, as lightning-struck, would fall—
Die, fever-smit, despite the will of Heaven.
"Was it crime-stained!" No she was friendless poor—
"Then poverty is crime?" Crime ! then the guileless
Nazarene was poor.
Had wealth enstamped it as of *finer* mould,
Though blotted with excess of revelry—
If lapped in down, like some gold jewelry,
Say, would the Christian here not paid his court,
And borne it softly in its velvet pall?
But *gold* is *worth*, in earth's false balance weighed:
Say, is gold current at the gate of heaven?
Or, *will it bribe the* terror-king to stay?

Get gold, or hire thee mourners ere you die,
It will, at least, a burial purchase thee,
Even though thou shouldst lie in a *stranger's grave.*
Had stained humanity not stretched her hand,
The very stones had lifted up their voice
To chide the charity that's ever kind,
The boast and glory of our *Christian* land.
Which here seemed fallen asleep, or journeying far,
Had closed her ready ear and pitying eye,
Folding in listlessness her open hand,
Nor heard the plaint of penury's wo-struck child,
Begging the last rite man e'er seeks of man—
The least tired clay begs of its fellow-clay,
Which common nature claims and nature owes,
By right of brotherhood and human law—
A hand to lay his helpless head in dust,
And hide the broken pitcher out of sight.
Though pity withheld her wonted prayer,
The "Man of sorrows" looked in mercy down.
A wretched group in pity gathered round—
The weary from his toil—the hungry hasting to his e
meal—
The fallen wretch, whom day had shamed to night—
The conscience-seared, whom want lured on to sin,
And like a gangrene froze all feeling's streams,
Now here a forgotten "touch of kin,"
And asked, "How did this one or parents sin?"
Till virtue's prodigal, long lost, looked back
A moment from the loathsome husks of sin,
With melting longings to their early home,

"And cursed religion as hypocrisy, when Israelites
Passed on the other side." There, too, I saw—
I heard, the meagre, pale-faced artisan,
Whose sinews labour sucked to withering;
His pale brow burned oft 'neath the sweat of sin—
Flushing with honest pride, where Nature's blood
Boiled up and rose to claim its family right
Of common brotherhood of equal clay—
"Humanity! assert your heaven-born right,"
Stretch forth your hands, "Here poverty is crime!"
Woman, last at the cross, first at the tomb,
Like good Samaritan, chaffed sorrow's wound.
Christian! go feed the hungry lest they sin;
The cause thou knowest not do *thou* seek out;
Nor let humanity e'er lift a stone,
To cast reproach on love that's ever kind—
On charity that seeketh not its own;
And wound that holy faith by which you're called,
That vows to love its neighbour as itself!

THE SANG O' THE SPINDLE.

The spindle, the only machine in olden times, with the simp and loom of home manufacture. The mode of counting the ha yarn is embodied in the unique "ower-come" of the following. simple tale of ingenious industry, may preserve the remembran piece of ancient cottage furniture—cast aside amid the lumber o days, but hanging like dusty pictures on the memories of our S grand-dames.

AULD Auntie was nae spinster bauld,
A leal-guid bodie she;
In the bonnie howe o' a heath'ry knowe,
Aside a broomy lea,
She calmly twined the thread o' life,
An' turned her reel about,
Singing, tu's ane—an' tu's no ane—
An' tu's twa a' oot.

She aft o' thriftie rockins spak',
O' cracks an' kempkins rare,
Where eident lasses blithely span
The lint as straight's a hair.
An' aye they twined their siller skene,
An' twirled the reel about,
Singing, tu's ane—and tu's no ane—
An' tu's twa a' oot.

An' orphan boy, her pride and joy,
A lammie in her e'e,
Played wi' the spindle at her feet,
Or wumpled 'bout her knee.
An' ower, an' ower, like Auntie's sang,
He read her ballad book,
Singing, tu's ane—an' tu's no ane—
An' tu's twa a' oot.

Near a dark tarn their sheilin lay,
'Mang druid rocks that hung
Cauld shadows ower its dowie face,
Like cluds ower winter's sun;
There up and down, the lang day roun',
He watched the water coot,
And learned its sang, had ower-come nane,
But aye the twa a' oot.

Then weel he watched ae wee pet lamb,
Or brought frae loaning green
The kye, frae 'mang the seggans lang,
To neebours hame at e'en.
Or paidled by the lochs an' burns,
To catch the wylie trout,
An' whiles got ane—an' whiles got nane—
An' whiles the twa a' oot.

His parent-tree wi' sheilin-bough,
By death was wede awa,
An' left alane, 'mang shaken leaves,
Ae wee *bit bud to* blaw.

But heaven casts, wi' tenty care,
  Love's downy lap about
The orphan lane, wha friends has nane,
  And maks the lost twa oot.

The helping han', in time o' need,
  Gets something aye to gi'e;
The gowd that's grasped wi' miser greed,
  Taks wings itsel' to flee.
And whiles the purse that's hespet steeve,
  Tines a' its gatherings oot,
An' catching ane—it whiles gets nane—
  And seldom twa a' oot.

A moral guid has Auntie's sang—
  This birring earth's a wheel,
We're spinners a', threads short or lang,
  Just as we spin, we reel.
An' up an' down, the thread o' life
  Has many a wheel about:
Noo—as we spin Time's gowden warp,
  Life's wab is woven out.

THE MOTHERLESS.

"A mother's fondness reigns without a rival."

All blessings guard the motherless!
They want that soothing rest,
That earnest love, so weariless,
That home—a mother's breast;
That love, with all its sunless wealth,
Of prayer, toil, and tears;
The only love that may not dread
The touch of earthly years;

That yearning faith, whose waveless deep
No swelling tide may change;
Whose hopeful watchings ne'er may sleep—
Whose look may ne'er grow strange;
The lamp, whose oil still quenchless burns,
Through long, long nights of pain,
Once quenched, its radiance ne'er returns
To light our path again.

When sickness pales the rosy cheek,
And clouds the sunny eye,
And on the wasting bed of pain
The weary head must lie;

O! who may soothe the fears of death,
With half the sleepless care,
Or warm our bosoms with the breath
That wings a mother's prayer.

When, from our early home, we pine
In stranger lands afar,
Still, through the darkest cloud may shine
One solitary star,
To woo us with a glad return
To home and kindred dear—
The hope that on our cheek may burn
Again—a mother's tear!

When links that bound the family band
Are broken o'er the ground,
And cares that strung a mother's hand
No more on earth are found:
O! who may chide the countless tears
That sacred spot would crave,
Or tell the voiceless memories
That haunt a mother's grave.

O! Thou in whose warm bosom blends
The wealth of earthly love;
Whose human nature tearful bends
To earth, from heaven above;
The Father of the fatherless,
The homeless orphan's stay,
O! guard and guide the *motherless*,
Through life's dark evil day!

"THE E'ENIN' FA'."

THE bee has left the closin' flower,
The lark the downy air;
An' saftly fa's the dewy hour,
That woos the heart frae care:
The choral sang o' joyfu' day,
In murmurs die awa';
The gowden blush, on burn an' brae,
Melts in our e'enin' fa'.

The e'enin' star blinks bonnilie,
To wyle the day awa';
Hope whispers in its sparkling e'e
O' rest at e'ein' fa';
Of hames afar o' peace an' light,
Where tempests never blaw,
Nor gatherin' shadows tell o' night,
Where comes *nae* e'enin' fa'.

Noo mithers seek the wander'd wean,
An' herds their roaming sheep,
Pale sorrow dauners oot alane,
O'er hapless waes to weep;

Amang the shades o' brighter days,
Weird memory melts awa',
And trims his lamp, wi' faded rays,
Alane at e'enin' fa'.

Frae burn an' brae the weary bairns,
Wi' wild flowers buskit braw,
Cower cannilie by haunted cairns,
Chased hame by e'enin' fa';
The corn-craik chirmeth eerilie,
Where nature's tear-draps fa';
An' gowans shut the dewy e'e,
To *sleep* at e'enin' fa'.

Noo plovers sing their wail-a-day,
Where heather blossoms blaw;
And downy mists row down the brae,
To hap the e'enin' fa'.
Noo slowly comes the hush divine,
O'er dusky glen an' shaw,
Sae like to heaven's walking time—
The *holy* e'enin' fa'.

The gudewife piles her e'enin' fire,
The bairns around it draw,
To welcome hame the weary sire,
Just at the e'enin' fa'.
The langest day wears to an end,
Earth's darkest night awa',—
To weary hearts and weary men,
How sweet the e'enin' fa' !

But, O! there's no a bonnier sight,
'Mang Scotland's hearths ava,
Than when, aneath their blinkin' light,
They kneel at e'enin' fa'.
For auld an' young maun bend the knee—
The servant, sire, an' a',
Pour forth the holy psalmody,
A' ane at e'enin' fa' !

An' weel I loe the e'enin' fire,
Where kind hearts gather a';
The blending tones o' voice an' lyre—
How sweet at e'enin' fa' !
To read auld stories o' the past,
O' friends neo far awa';
The faces covered wi' Time's blast
We *miss* at e'enin' fa'.

Kind pity shield the beggar lane,
An' wash his weary feet;
O! sweep for him the warm hearth-stane,
Wha sorrow's crumbs maun eat;
The wand'rer, wha sair burdened ben's
'Mang poortith's drifting snaw—
The feckless, wha nae body kens—
Hameless, at e'enin' fa' !

O! when our sun gaes to its bed,
An' daylight creeps awa',
May Hope's pure star its glory shed,
Around our e'enin' fa';

A friendly hand to close my e'e,
  Night's curtains round me draw,
An' drap a burning tear o'er me,
  Unseen, at e'enin' fa'.

ALICE BLAND.

"'Twas mournful to sit by her pillow, and mark
  The paleness that dwelt on her cheek,
Her cold marble brow, with its ringlets so dark,
  Her patience so holy and meek."

BEND, brother, o'er that form, and weep,
  For death's pale, chilly hand,
Hath reft the roses from the cheek
  Of lovely Alice Bland.

Those features, mutely eloquent—
  That lofty marblo brow—
Each soul-expressive lineament,
  Is cold and callous now.

Her eye of blue, her soul-lit eye,
  Her sweet and sunny smile,
Could chase away the mourner's sigh,
  And all his woes beguile.

Now, there no soft emotions beam,
  Nor smile, nor tear, nor sighs;
In marble beauty, cold serene,
  Pale, passionless, she lies.

She sleepeth, in her dreamless rest,
  Far from her kindred land;
The cold turf wraps the virgin breast
  Of lovely Alice Bland.

Amid the glory-gilded blooms
  Of yonder happy land,
A heavenly radiance illumes
  The shade of Alice Bland.

FADING BEAUTY.

"Ah! such the change the heart displays,
So frail is early friendship's reign."

"The last rose of summer"
Has sighed its decay,
The sear leaves of autumn
Are passing away;
Now songless the valleys,
And leafless the trees;
No flowers in the woodland—
No balm on the breeze;
The bright sky is changing
Its shining array
Of purple and gold
For a mantle of grey.
As the snow on the mountain,
The ice on the rill,
So love's glowing fountain
Grows callous and chill.
The sunshine of friendship
Whose soul-cheering ray
Lit the heart with its brightness,
Is passing away!

Oh! all, all is changing
  In this changing scene;
But, oh! shall our friends be
  As they had ne'er been?
Are the friends whom we cherish
  All faithfully true?
"Gay hearts are many,
  Sincere ones are few."
The cherished are changing—
  The fond, where are they?
Oh! life, love, and beauty,
  Like flowers ye decay!

THE BROKEN HEART.

"She died in beauty, like a rose
Blown from its parent stem."

ONE passed away like a morning cloud,
In golden light, to the voiceless shroud,
Her cheek had still its rose-leaf bloom,
When they bore her away to the sunless tomb;
And her eye was bright as dew on flowers,
In the diamond sheen of moonlight hours.
The life-lamp died when its flame was bright,
Nor smouldered away in a waning light.
She laid her head on her mother's breast,
And sung herself like a babe to rest;
And thought went out from her radiant eye,
When the life-cord snapt in a broken sigh;
And they marvelled why she passed away
Without a shade of dark decay;
For death, as a smiling masquer, came
With syren song, with no frown of pain.
And the flowers she gathered were not dead
When strewn on the white funereal bed—

Where she lay so pale, so cold, so still,
Like the sleeping song of a frozen rill.
But one who knew what young hearts bear—
The voiceless pain and the viewless care,—
When the big grief-ache, which tongue ne'er tells,
In the weary heart to breaking swells,
With the venomed blight of affection's sting,
Which she, dove-like, covers with silken wing,
Cow'ring 'mid leaves in its downy nest,
To still the beat of its trembling breast—
Covering the barb of the broken dart,
To hide the wound of the bleeding heart,
Till it sighs out its life in a low sweet tone,
Like the moanings soft of the wind-harp's song,—
"That she trembled to hear one hoarded name,
Yet seemed to con it o'er again."
When they spoke of one beyond the sea,
Her breath came thick and "doubtingly;"
And it flushed on her cheek that little word,
Like the heart of a rose, which the wind has stirred;
But it oft turned pale, and she seemed to grieve
'Mid the fading light, when the star of eve,
And its beaming kin, came one by one,—
And she wept to watch them all alone,
Then stole to a casket, where gems lay hid
In a lock of hair; when she raised the lid
The heart, overfull, gushed free, and proved,
By the sob and the tear, how deep she loved.
But the snowdrop springs on her grassy bed,
Where young hearts weep and shake the head,

When they read the date on the white grave-stone—
That the bloom was nipt e'er the flower was blown—
That she left her loved in her sunlight hours,
'Mid the song of birds and awaking flowers;
Like a silver star on the brow of day,
In the growing light of the dawning ray;
And her soul's deep love, with its voiceless trust,
She hid it low in the secret dust.
And one who could read the mystic leaf
In the folded book of woman's grief,
And could trace the tears when fond hearts part,
Whispered, "She died of a broken heart."

Wo for those who from earth depart,
Bearing no pangs of the "Broken Heart."

ON THE DEATH OF LADY FLORA HASTINGS.

"Peace to her broken heart and virgin grave."

WHY is there wailing in yon princely hall?
There every heart is sad—each voice is low;
There one is wrapt in death's funereal pall;
There, heart-wrung tears, in burning torrents, flow:
The silent marble echoes back the sighs,
Convulsing every breast of every weeper;
Mute, bending o'er the virgin form, that lies
In marble death, a calm, a dreamless sleeper.

The spirit-withering, upas-breathing blight
Of poisoning falsehood's pestilential breath,
That scorches with the dire sirocco's might,
Withered that pure and injured flower to death.
Calumniators, with the hearts of stone!
While she, on high, the song of victory sings,
Here is a picture you must gaze upon,
And feel how deep the serpent, conscience, stings.
Oh! if ye sink unpardoned 'neath the sod
On earth, Eternal Justice shall arraign
Your perjured spirits at the bar of God,
To bide the audit here she sought in vain.

Behold her to the cemetery borne,
  In silent sorrow, on the sable bier,
Where hundreds over worth departed mourn,
  And drop o'er injured innocence a tear.
Upon her bosom snow-white flowers are laid—
  The emblems meet of innocence and love—
The deathless wreath of flowers that never fade,
  And garland the immortal brow above!
See her laid gently in her last repose;
  Her friends seem envying her stirless rest:
Ah! who may tell the agonising woes
  That wrings the brothers', sisters', parents' breast.

She lieth low, in life's meridian hour,
  A martyred victim to the silent tomb—
A crushed, a broken, and a blighted flower,
  Nipt in the acme of her being's bloom;
But, when the cerements of the tomb are riven,
  That form, enrobed in innocence, shall rise
Pure as the soul "imparadised in heaven,"
  Before the assembled world's admiring eyes.

What though of calumny she bore the frown!
  It sped her progress to the courts of bliss;
And for a cross she has received a crown,
  And nobly conquered—conquered, yea, in this.

THE SONG OF SPRING.

> "The woods shall hear the voice of Spring,
> And flourish green again."

THE dwellers in the woodland
Have heard the voice of Spring,
And, pouring star-born melody,
The lark is on the wing.
A gush of songful music
Is bursting with the rills;
The tuneful notes of gladd'ning life
Are floating o'er the hills;
The noon-light clouds fling beauty
O'er earth from laughing skies,
And mirror on her blooming breast
Their rainbow-tainted dyes;
The glowing breezes waken
The children of the earth,
And fan the cradled seeds of life
That feed the flowret's birth;
The green unfolding leaflets,
In bud and bough unsealed,
Shall flush her face with blossom,
When their beauty is revealed,

And weave a broidered vesture,
  And twine festoons of flowers
To decorate her bosom,
  And garland summer bowers.
O! what a marvellous power is hid
  Within an atom seed,
That bears the stream of teeming life
  O'er mountain, vale, and mead;
The secret graves of dark decay,
  With strength and beauty fills
The fountain of unnumbered springs,
  That feed her myriad rills,
Till "downy buds" of silken leaves
  Are flung in blossom showers,
Where sunshine warms her frozen breast,
  And leads the beaming hours;
The rosy lights are falling
  At gorgeous even time—
The prophecy of cloudless skies,
  In summer's leafy prime;
The insect brood are creeping
  From their wintry shroud of clay,
Outspreading silver-tissued wings
  To sport in golden day.
Let sorrow doff her sable weeds,
  And seek the breezy hill,
Till nature's smiling loveliness
  The heart with joyance fill,
And sickness woo the gentle breath
  Of the awak'ning flowers,

The pale cheek gather fresh'ning bloom
From hope-inspiring hours.
For soon the bee will hum his song
'Mid blossom-laden boughs,
Their dancing leaves hold dalliance
With the blushing purple rose;
The school-boy carrols like a bird,
Far in the quiet vale,
Amid the wild-rose, brake, or fern,
To seek the primrose pale,
To watch the silver willows play,
With foam-bell on the brooks,
Where babbling waters wandering stray
Through violet-tufted nooks.
O! what would light the wintry chill
Of life's unnumbered woes,
Did faith not hope a future spring—
A home-land of repose;
The fragrance of the spring-tide flowers,
In budding beauty bright,
Would shadow forth the dawning power
Of hope's divulging light—
The efflux of Eternal Mind,
Transfused through nature's frame
In all creation, issues forth
To laud his wondrous name;
And in existence multiform,
His all-pervading soul—
A guiding pulse—beats equably
Throughout the wondrous whole;

Pure from that deep, unfathomed Font—
  The centre spring—there streams
The flood of beauty, power, and love
  With which creation teems :
It radiates in the glorious sun—
  Breathes in the atom fly,
And gleams out in the pearl-shell
  Where ocean-treasures lie;
It thunders in the raven cloud
  Whose scathing wing of fire
Bows low the forest's Anak sons,
  And tears their leafy tire;
It burneth in the star of eve
  That lights devotion's hour,
And blushes in the velvet leaves
  Of the unfolding flower.

THE ROSE OF L——.

"'Tis an emblem of beauty, an emblem of love,
An emblem of virtue that blossoms above,
When the fading hues of beauty die
In the sunshine of immortality."

MEET emblem of thy owner,
Breathing all around perfume,
In all the flush of beauty,
In nature's sweetest bloom;
Distilling gentle odours
On the glad or fainting heart,
To all, the fragrancy of joy,
Her balmy words impart,
As leaf by leaf the new-born flower
Is blushing forth unseen,
And spreading out its balmy sweets
Beneath its shade of green.
'Tis thus the beauties of her mind,
Unfolding day by day,
Are wreathing it with loveliness
That cannot fade away—

Nursing those gentle charities
  That glowing hearts unfold,
Those tender sympathies of soul,
  By silence only told—
Those cords which close and closer draw
  Congenial mind to mind,
The finer feelings fondly with
  Our heart-strings intertwined;
Those tender ties, on which are hung
  The harmonies of life,
Whose music soothes our heart with song,
  Amid the jarring strife.
The pressure of the hand, a smile,
  A tone, a look, a word,
Are keys by which the deepest notes
  Within our hearts are stirred;
Whose tones the slightest touch may wake,
  As if by magic spell,
To conjure up our absent ones—
  The friends we love so well.
A curl of hair, a ring, a flower,
  A leaf may be the token,
That seals our love inviolate,
  Through long, long years unbroken.
O, friendship! faithful friendship,
  Is a high—a sacred thing,
The fountain whence unnumbered streams
  Of sweetest pleasure spring;
The earth is fresh and green where'er
  It sparkles o'er our way,

Cheering the weary traveller,
With flowers and melody;
It makes an oasis in the wild,
Where'er its waters flow,
The only earthly palmy ground
Amid this waste of wo—
The only shady spot whereon
The pilgrim heart may rest,
To lave the burning brow, and cool
The fever of the breast.
O! what were life without a friend?
A round of heartless joys—
A crowd of smiling mockeries,
Satiety destroys.
Soon as the gilded mask is thrown
In secrecy aside,
How fragile are the reeds whereon
Our human hopes relied.
Earth were an Egypt-land of plagues—
Of darkness, death, and doom—
Where peace-destroying angels make
Our home a living tomb;
Did not the guiding angel come,
And sprinkle o'er the heart
The type of everlasting love—
Of hopes that ne'er depart.
And virtue is that spirit light,
Fed from the golden urn,
That holds the oil of love by which
Our olive lamps must burn;

For, what were beauty's gorgeous bloom
  Without religion's power?
A soulless image, void of thought—
  A fair, a scentless flower.
Unlike that rose, its leaves may fade,
  Its beauty pass away,
But virtue's fragrance never dies—
  Its sweets outlive decay.
And time will blanch the fairest cheek,
  And blight the summer rose,
But, can the chilling night of death,
  The op'ning graces close
Of mind—of evergrowing mind—
  That burns and radiates still,
Even when the broken censer lies
  In dust all pale and chill;
Like her who tends thee, lovely flower,
  With beauty, virtue, crowned,
Now pouring rich benevolence
  On all who her surround.
Pale penury doth daily bless
  Her hand outstretched to save,
Her memory shall like odour rise
  Above the wasting grave.

TIME CHANGES.

"Change walks on both sides of this human life,
Its sunshine and its shadow."

"The summer has its heavy cloud,
The rose-leaf will fall."

O! MANY a sun in light has set,
And gold of summer eves,
And many a rose, since last we met,
Has shed its budding leaves—
Leaves in the flush of spring-tide bloom,
Are scattered far, and sere;
And young hearts o'er the shrouding tomb
Have poured the parting tear.

Ay! green leaves from unshaken boughs,
Are fading in the dust;
And summer flowers, and winter snows,
Conceal the young heart's trust,—
Loved voices, with their kindly tone,
And sweet, familiar face,
From friendship's smiling circle gone,
And left "a vacant place."

Stars, that in beauty lit our night,
Away in light have passed;
And eyes, in hope's effulgence bright,
On loved ones looked their last;

Hearts that have rushed in bounding glow,
To meet a sister heart,
Like mountain streams their mingled flow
Is dried, or far apart.

And we, around our hearts, have twined
Affections rich and new;
The early dear are still as kind,
And O! how deeply true.
And who remembers life's young hour,
Where first-affections blend,
Nor feels the soul o'er-mastering power
That wraps an early friend?

When rushing back, with miser care,
We count youth's golden store,
And paint again the pictures fair,
Heart-framed in days of yore;
For memory's crystal graven urn,
Ashes and gems may hold,
Where fires, long quenched, may smould'ring burn
With strifes to earth untold.

And change has waved across our way,
A light and heavy wing;
And sun and shadow marked our day,
With joy and sorrowing;
But still we hold a changeless trust—
A hope that never dies;
'Twill shine when all of earth is dust,
Beyond these fading skies.

'TIS WHISPERED THOU ART SAD.

I NEVER deemed thee sorrowful—
  I thought you glad and gay,
Thy life a dream of song and flowers—
  A golden summer day;
I never dreamed a sorrow slept
  Beneath the smile you wore—
I never thought so warm a heart
  Was bleeding at the core.
And when I saw thee dance and sing,
  I thought thee truly glad—
A young, a bright, a happy thing,—
  How could I deem thee sad?
And if a silver cloud should dim
  The brightness of thine eyes,
Methinks it soon may pass away,
  Like clouds from summer skies.
I gaze on thy expressive face,
  I trace its every line,
Methinks I see a something there
  I cannot well define;
And then there comes a withering thought,
  Like fever through my brain,—
Oh, agony!—that sunny smile
  May hide a secret pain.

O, would that I could read thy soul
  Beneath that veil of gladness!
For, ah! methinks thy spirit wears
  A pensive tone of sadness;—
I know not—would that I could know!
  The feelings you conceal
From me, as from a heartless one,
  Who does not, cannot feel.
I gaze upon thy smiling brow,
  And roses 'mid thy hair,
Then tell me, how can I believe
  A shadow lingers there?
They say there's sorrow in thy soul
  When thou art all alone,—
O, would that joy were only thine,
  That grief were mine alone!
And if I must not, cannot know,
  Your feelings, doubts, and fears,
Or when thy cheek is flushed with joy,
  Or pale with secret tears;
Oh! when the silver stars are clear,
  "And vesper shuts the rose,"
And myriads of human kind
  Are wrapt in deep repose:
I'll breathe the fervid orison,
  Low on my bended knee—
Oh! then how fervently I'll plead
  For happiness to thee.

"LOST TO SIGHT, TO THOUGHT HOW DEAR!"

(THE MOTTO OF A SEAL.)

"Lost to sight, to thought how dear!"
Set a seal upon my heart,
I would have thee ever near,
Where no changes ever part.

"Lost to sight, to thought how dear!"
Oft my spirit leans on thine;
Oft you whisper in mine ear,
Peace! when tempted to repine.

"Lost to sight, to thought how dear!"
Thy sweet spirit, gentle, kind,
Communes softly with me here,
In the chambers of the mind.

"Lost to sight, to thought how dear!"
Time or distance cannot part
Bonds, which draw you nearer, near,
Close and closer to my heart.

"THE LIGHT OF OTHER DAYS."

THE clouds of "other days" have faded,
And all their darkness past;
And peace, with golden wing, has shaded
The hopes too vain to last.

Like morning breaking on the ruin,
The shadows flee away,
And the "joy of love" the heart is wooing,
With the "Light of other days."

The flowers that earthly tempests wither,
Are swept by death's cold blast,
But the "Rose of Sharon" blooms for ever,
When life's short day is past.

The morning star of peace, unclouded,
Shines forth with purest ray;
And the heart now feels, where sorrow shrouded,
"The light of other days."

THE POWER OF GENIUS.

Who has not bowed beneath the master power
Of heaven-born genius, that immortal dower,
Investing thought with all-enduring birth,
And, as a mighty lever, moving earth;
Nerving those myriad energies of mind
That circle through the mass of human kind,
Swaying their actions like a mighty soul,
And ruling millions with unseen control?
Who has not knelt before the heaven-lit shrine,
  And marvelled at its ruling mastery;
Soared on the lightning wing of thought sublime,
  Or trembled 'neath its magic potency?
Been spell-bound 'neath a gush of sorcery sounds,
  When tides of eloquence in music flows,
Till every fibre in our bosom bounds,
  And, awed to ecstacy, the spirit glows?
By genius' hand the cloudy veil is riven,
  That heaven's starry, burning glories hide;
By it we track the wilderness of heaven,
  Where circling worlds round worlds circling glide.
'Tis hers to scan, by Science's Argus eye,
  The mystic glories of each wandering star;
And charm the viewless planets from the skies,
  That shine in empyrean depths afar.
'Tis by the alchemy of master-mind
The gold of thought is seven times refined,

Melted and analyzed by genius' flame,
In the laboratory of the brain—
Which, in that crucible of earthen mould,
Transmutes the very dust to gems and gold,
The existing forms of matter she transforms—
  The chain that binds the elements dissolve;
And from the wreck a new creation forms,
  Whence Science's mighty principles evolve,
By these unveiling, that we clearly trace
The hidden lineaments of nature's face;
  Have you not traced the godlike in the creature,
When the eye flashes out the sp'rit-ray;
  And on the ample brow and lofty feature
The expressive thoughts of genius richly play?
Imagination, in his silver car,
Then rolls amid the fiery spheres from star to star:
  Soars high upon her richly-coloured wings,
Searching the depths of ocean, earth, and sky,—
  Gathering the substance of all glorious things
Where'er the elements of beauty lie,
  To decorate sublime imaginings.
'Tis then the arm of intellect on high
  Is raised, to grasp the impalpable thought,
And drag the floating phantom from the sky,—
  Then, mastered and condensed, to earth is brought
The flitting coruscation of the mind;
  And language fetters down the lightning glance,
Bestows it as a gift to human kind—
  A permanent, a rich inheritance.

HE DIED ALONE.

ON THE DEATH OF A PROMISING YOUNG MAN, WHO DIED SUDDENLY AT A DISTANCE FROM HIS FRIENDS.

No mother, in his agony, bent o'er him,
To wipe the dew of death with gentle hand,
No sire—for they had gone to death before him;
He died 'mid strangers, in a stranger land.
No kindred band around his bed were weeping,
To whom he might love's yearning wishes tell,
To breathe a prayer, while yet the soul was fleeting,
Or soothe the anguish of the last farewell!

He suffered perils on the stormy tide,
And clung, 'mid terrors to the sinking wreck,
When death's devouring jaws were yawning wide,
As if to tear him from the shattered deck.
He braved and buffeted the foaming billow,
When the wild war of waters thundered high,
And then he laid him on the stranger's pillow,
No friend, no brother near to close his eye.

His body lies not in the nameless grave,
Where heaves no sigh, no holy requiem swells,
Where the long sea weeds wreath the coral caves,
'Neath the blue wave, amid the silver shells!

But they have wrapt him in his parent earth,
Hushed in the silence of the green churchyard,
Where friends who watched his boyhood's gleesome mirth,
With bleeding hearts his ashes may regard.

Where every tombstone is a finger post,
Pointing the pilgrim to his journey's end,
Where he will meet the friends on earth he lost,
Where all our joys and woes in peace shall blend.
Though op'ning fair in dawning manhood's prime,
The buds of promise wreathed his youthful brow,
The type of golden fruits in after time,
Are buried in the dust and scattered now !

He wrestled with disease 'neath India's sun,
And fearless braved the darkling ocean gale,
But now his earthly sand is quickly run,
Fate cast his anchor in the peaceful vale.
Death is our heir-loom, and the meed of sin,
That schools vain men to seek the immortal prize—
To press towards the crowning mark, and win
The fadeless palm—the life that never dies !

THE FIRST-BORN.

"The infant mind as wax will take
  Impressions of the finest mould;
But Satan draws in many a shape
  His image on the tarnished gold."

BUD of many hopes and fears!
  The first, the elder born;
Thy *life's* unwritten leaf appears
A folded tale of smiles and tears,
Sealed in the book of future years,
  Unopened, yet untorn.

Now in affection's lap carest,
  "A mystery thou art;"
Eternity sleeps in thy breast,
Though here a wandering stream at best—
A tide of calm or dark unrest,
  Lies fountained in thy heart.

Germ of a life that never dies;
  A dower of wealth untold;
That stem a rod of strength may rise—
A tare—a flower of Paradise—
A temple-vessel for the skies,
  From youth's unmolten gold.

And though no visioned eye may see
  Life's folded roll, to tell
What in its pictured page may be,
Of shade or sunshine writ for thee,
Still Hope would paint a prophecy
  That yet to truth may swell.

May thy fond mother never know
  A mother's bitter tears;
With God and man in favour grow—
Ne'er may you quench the yearning glow
Of love, whose streams of care now flow,
  To watch thy coming years.

Thy father's staff, thy mother's stay,
  Till calm they sleep in dust;
May disappointment ne'er betray,
By sudden blight or slow decay,
The flower, long watchings night and day,
  To hopeful bloom had nurst.

While on that smiling face of thine,
  In reflex rays we trace,
Still miniature, the features fine,
The growing, blending parent line;
May truth, to perfect form sublime
  Within each spirit grace.

TO A FRIEND ON HER BIRTH-DAY.

"Grow in grace and in the knowledge of our Lord and Sa
Jesus Christ."

THY heart is in its spring-tide, full and flowing,
Warm, sparkling in the sunny light of youth;
A deep-hued rose-bud, rich in beauty blowing,
And odour-full of sacred love and truth,
Out-welling in the hush of even-time,
In heaven-poured breathings—orisons and praise;
Drinking unfolding light, in morning's prime,
From the eternal sun's life-giving rays:
O! guard it—canker creeps o'er sweetest flowers,
And tears will bend it, in thy cloudy hours.

Thy life is in its spring-time, opening green—
A lovelier leaf unfolding day by day,
The fruits of faith and charity serene,
Growing and ripening in thy upward way;
And though the fruitage branch with blossom swells,
Yet droughts may come to thee, that come to all:
O! thou must draw deep from "salvation's wells,"
E'er thy full harvest golden shadows fall.
And who may tell of buds beneath the skies
What their full bloom may be in Paradise!

Thy hopes are in their morning, crimson-bright
  Penciling with radiance thy future sky,
Piercing the clouds with rays of heavenly light,
  And drawing scenes of joy that never die;
But earth-born mists may dim thy views of heaven;
  For still, with sin-born fears, dark nature teems:
Then plead that purifying light be given,
  Reflected from the Cross, in guiding beams,
To chase the shadows when temptations frown,
And show beyond the stars the blood-bought crown.

The heart of thought and action is the spring,
  Tinging the stream of all life's ruling feelings;
O! keep it well, it is a subtle thing!
  Temper, by conquering Truth, its meek revealings.
And life is "fading as the flower of grass;"
  Then cleave, by faith, unto the living Vine,
That, though thy years "e'en as a shadow pass,"
  Still wear the glorious robe of Love divine—
Then Hope, in its fruition, shall excel
More, more than eye hath seen or heart can tell!

STANZAS.

"Things which are seen are temporal."

I ENVY not!—I covet not—
 The world's meed of fame:
I would not use a latent power
 To win a laureled name.

I covet not the shining store
 Of wealth's delusive joys;—
What care I for its glittering ore,
 Its tinselry, and toys!

Ambition's roses will decay,
 Its amaranthine flowers!
The palm of glory fades away
 In fame's meridian hours.

And what is glory—but a dream,
 To cheat the aching sight;
The flitting of a meteor-gleam,
 A momentary light!

Fame—'tis a mockery refined,
 To deck the poet's grave,
It undulates with every mind,
 Like moonbeams on the wave.

And friendship is a fading flower,
  Reserve may soon destroy;
A word may wither in one hour
  That bud of earthly joy.

Then what can fill immortal mind,
  In climes so poor as this,
But *Truth* eternal and refined,
  Yea, soul-enduring bliss.

THE PHILOSOPHER.

Respectfully Inscribed to T. Morton, Esq., H.M.R.S.S.A.

"He plants the wire where grow the Tyrian leaves,
Whence industry her pictured tissue weaves."

THOUGH science clothe him in her mantle sage,
Sun-eyed philosophy his thoughts engage,
He shines the radii of a circle fair,
Whose lines of beauty sweet reflections bear;
His children find a playmate in their sire,
Child-like in love, beside the evening fire.
His spirit warm, unchilled by frigid art,
His open hand an echo of his heart;
Nor pity woos in vain his ready ear—
His hand would rather wipe than force the tear;
In manners simple, and in taste refined,
"A cunning workman," whose ingenious mind
A second vision to the eye conveys,
And pictures near the distant planet's blaze;
Gathering, from heaven's far wilderness of light,
The golden sands that strew the plains of night,
Drawing, with magic glass, the jewels down,
That star with majesty her silver crown;
While peopled atoms into worlds turn,
And specs in air as suns and systems burn,
Like winged seraphim that travels space,
Reveal the glory of their Author's face,
In rays of Deity still sparkling through
The temple veils of the eternal blue.

SUMMER.

"The flowers appear on the earth."

It is summer—oh, 'tis summer!
There is music in the trees,
And sunshine on the crystal rills—
There's perfume on the breeze.

The curtains of the sky are hung
In many a graceful fold;
A rich, a gorgeous drapery,
Of mingled blue and gold.

And Sol is pouring from on high
Effulgence pure and bright,
And deluging this nether sphere
With floods of amber light.

'Tis ecstacy to linger now
Amid the garden bowers,
To wander 'neath a sunny sky,
And drink the breath of flowers.

Sweet Flora cometh, scattering balm,
Upon her silken wings;
And on the bosom of the earth
Her flowery mantle flings.

I'll even be a worshipper
In nature's holy shrine;
In all her glorious lineaments
I trace a hand divine.

But nature offers sacrifice
More pure and deep than ours,
From twice ten thousand golden cups
Of incense-breathing flowers.

THE AULD KIKK-YARD.

"Where heaved the turf in many a mouldering heap."

CALM sleep the village dead,
  In the auld kirk-yard;
But softly, slowly, tread,
  In the auld kirk-yard;
For the weary, weary, rest,
Wi' the green turf on their breast,
And the ashes o' the blest
  Flower the auld kirk-yard.

It has a wrinkled face,
  The auld kirk-yard;
And tears, of years, we trace
  In the auld kirk-yard;
Strifes, to the earth unknown,
Revealed to God alone,
Hid, by the tribute stone,
  In the auld kirk-yard.

Oh! many a tale it hath,
  The auld kirk-yard,
Of life's crooked, thorny path
  To the auld kirk-yard.

But mortality's thick gloom
Clouds the sunny world's bloom,
Veils the mystery of doom,
In the auld kirk-yard.

A thousand memories spring,
In the auld kirk-yard,
Though Time's death-brooding wing
Shade the auld kirk-yard.
The light of many a hearth,
Its music and its mirth,
Sleep in the deep dark earth
Of the auld kirk-yard.

Nae dreams disturb their sleep,
In the auld kirk-yard;
They hear nae kindred weep,
In the auld kirk-yard.
The sire, with silver hair;
The mother's heart of care;
The young, the gay, the fair,
Crowd the auld kirk-yard.

'Tis a chamber for the bride
Oft, the auld kirk-yard;
A shroud for beauty's pride,
The auld kirk-yard.
On the haughty lip of rose
The greedy worms repose,
Where the lowly gowan blows,
In the auld kirk-yard.

There's nae kind voice of friend
  In the auld kirk-yard;
Hearts meet, but cannot blend,
  In the auld kirk-yard;
Nae song o' joy to cheer,
Nae hand to wipe a tear,
Nae pale foreboding fear,
  In the auld kirk-yard.

They hear nae Sabbath bell
  In the auld kirk-yard;
Nae voice of hope to tell
  In the auld kirk-yard;
Though holy music falls
Around the auld kirk walls,
Nae voice of mercy calls
  To the auld kirk-yard.

They hear nae tale of wo
  In the auld kirk-yard;
They fear nae serpent foe
  In the auld kirk-yard;
Nae smooth deceitful smile,
Nae honied lip o' guile,
Nae hunger, pain, or toil,
  In the auld kirk-yard.

They sing nae ev'ning psalm
  In the auld kirk-yard;
Nae prayer sheds its balm
  In the auld kirk-yard,

Nor holy man of God
Pours the dew-drops of the Word
On the ears beneath the sward,
  In the auld kirk-yard.

Life's greenest leaf lies low
  In the auld kirk-yard;
Swept from the giant bough,
  To the auld kirk-yard;
And the sere leaf 'neath our tread
Whispers, o'er the dreamless dead,
As a leaf we all do fade
  To the auld kirk-yard.

The gorgeous starlight gleams
  On the auld kirk-yard;
And spring-time's fostering beams
  Gild the auld kirk-yard;
But the lang, lang winter snows
A wreathy mantle throws
O'er the sere and blighted rose
  In the auld kirk-yard.

But the heart's sad beatings cease
  In the auld kirk-yard:
And aliens rest in peace
  In the auld kirk-yard.
Where ebbed dark floods of strife
Dove-like Hope, wi' promise rife,
Plants the broken branch o' life
  In the auld kirk-yard.

Read our covenant fathers' faith
  In the auld kirk-yard;
On the chronicles o' death,
  In the auld kirk-yard.
See the Bible and the sword,
O'er the persecuting hoard,
Tell the triumphs o' the Lord,
  In the auld kirk-yard.

By yon rudely-lettered stone,
  In the auld kirk-yard,
Bend thy spirit's holiest tone,
  In the auld kirk-yard.
Where the long grass rankly waves
O'er the holy martyr's grave,
Pour the solemn meed it craves,
  In the auld kirk-yard.

They were chased by sin-girt men,
  Frae the auld kirk-yard,
To the mountain an' the glen,
  Near the auld kirk-yard—
The mossy cave their bed,
Where the waving fern, o'erspread,
Only canopied their head,
  Near the auld kirk-yard.

But the bluidy, bluidy sword,
  For their auld kirk-yard;
"Like water, poured their blood,"
  In that auld kirk-yard;

But it richly flowered the heath
Wi' the witness blooms o' faith,
And chased the tyrant's wrath
  To the auld kirk-yard.

So live that ye may lie,
  In the auld kirk-yard,
Wi' a passport to the sky,
  Frae the auld kirk-yard;
That when thy sand is run,
And life's weary warfare done,
Ye may sing o' victory won,
  Where there's nae kirk-yard.

SACRED LYRICS.

"Words, melting low in streams of sympathy,
In weakness 'fitly spoken' may not die
On Reason's ear, though sinking silently.
Dew to the heart are tear drops in the eye;
Thus thought with thought communing secretly,
Long 'mid the mountain-springs of mind may lie,
The pilgrim-drops that swell her rivers vast,
Lost 'mid the ocean-beds of memory.
One thought may 'travel through eternity'—
One drop may fill the cup of charity,
In Faith's alembic cast."

SACRED LYRICS.

"The voice of Truth,
Though trembling from a censer made of clay,
Where mercy spreads her angel-ministry,
May touch even lips unclean with sacred fire,
And music draw from marble, mute the lyre
In the 'veiled soul,' until the spirit ray
Awake thought's hidden chords to harmony.
Soulless and songless sleeps the ivory key,
Its 'liquid breath' a wand'ring melody;
Till light's soft fingers o'er its chaos stray,
Like Memnon's harp, its soul to worship given,
Attuned to love, in song *may* rise to heaven."

SACRED MUSIC.

"O! consecrate my life,
That I may sing of thee with joy, that hath a living spring,
In a full heart of music."

TRIUMPHANT music! raptly swells
In adoration's breathing tone,
And thrilling on the spirit, dwells
Like holy harpings round the throne;
The melting cadence trembles low,
In hallelujahs fades and dies,
Just like a soul about to go,
And burst in higher melodies.

As skylark on its dewy wing,
While soaring, singing, leaves the clod,
And at the gate of heaven sings,
And warbles in the ear of God.
O! thus to soar above the clouds
That dim our sight of sunless day,
And mingle with the adoring crowds
Who "dwell in love" and melody.

When praise upon our spirits float,
For endless song it inly sighs;
And, O! 'tis but a wand'ring note
From heaven's eternal melodies.
If thus a treasured earthly tone,
Stir the full heart so thrillingly,
When soul, and song, and voice are one,
What must the heavenly anthem be?

If we would sing in harmony,
Where heart-strings feel no jarring chord,
We must be absent from the clay,
And "ever present with the Lord;"
And hear, as John on Patmos heard,
"Like voice of many waters" rise,
The praises of the "Eternal Word"—
The angel-harpings of the skies.

Here we must touch with gentle hand,
The jarring chords of earthly strife,
And strike the notes on which depend
The heaven-taught harmonies of life.

THE LAST HYMN.

"Cease fond nature, cease thy strife,
And let me languish into life."

O! SING once more before I go,
That old familiar hymn,
With Sabbath tone, so sweet and low,
Ere morning songs begin.
Sing of the love that never dies,
The friends who never part,
Ere earthly love in silence lies,
While leaning on thy heart.
O! sing that holy hymn.

I learned it at my mother's knee,
And sung it to my sire;
And I have sung it oft with thee,
Beside our ev'ning fire;
Like odour from a faded rose,
'Twill breathe of beauty gone,—
Sing, ere earth's twilight shadows close,
For hearts must die alone.
Sing low that parting song.

Of faith's adoring mastery,
A victor crowned in dust,
That love's triumphant agony,
Which seals our meeting trust;
When broken is the golden bowl,
The silver cord is riven,
Of One who binds the widowed soul—
One, only One in Heaven;
To Him our song be given.

The ocean shell, though distant, sings
The music of the wave,
And sanctified affection springs
In song beyond the grave;
The Star that led us all our way,
Whose light I praised with thee,
Which lit our path with pillar-ray,
Thou'lt sing where is "no sea."
Of all that light with me.

Then touch my heart no more with gloom,
Of passionate farewells,
For through the love-illumin'd tomb
A flood of glory swells;
I hear ONE calling me by name,
"Thou'rt mine, I've ransom'd thee—
Fear not, I'm with thee in the flame,
I Seba gave for thee."
Hush! hush! my loved one, see!

I come, like the o'er-wearied dove,
  My ark, my covenant home;
O! clasp me in the arms of love,
  O'er floods no more to roam.
But, hark! the angel-chorals swell,
  Sing, glory! glory, sing!
O grave! where is thy victory, tell,
  And where, O! death, thy sting?
        Earth! earth! dim earth, farewell!

"NO NIGHT THERE."

INSCRIBED TO ——

"But the throne of God and the Lamb shall be in it."—Rev. xxi. 5.

NIGHT soon falls with wan decline
O'er the light and bloom of earth's fairest time,
And coldness creeps, like a wintry day,
O'er the young hearts bounding, burning play;
Tear-drops shadow our sunny hours,
Frequent as dew on closing flowers ;
And silence comes with parting breath,
Sealing the lip with the image of death.
When shadows of dark forgetfulness cloud
The spirit's light with a voiceless shroud,
And sleep, with her dreamy pictures, lie
As a veil of mist on the starry eye.
When the sparkling tide of life lies still,
As music-foam on a frozen rill—
And separation mutely lies,
On the spirit's answering harmonies.
Fitful and few, in this vale of night,
Are the wand'ring rays of pilgrim-light—

Their heaven-born sheen all featly pass,
Like morning dews, or moonlit glass;
Like hermit-stars, burn faint and dim,
In clouding mist of dark'ning sin;
And our feeble love grows cold and dark
With the waring thought of the faithless heart.
No night is there—no day's decline—
No shadows darken that blissful clime—
No waning moon—no sunless day—
No clouds on the light of eternity—
Nor dews—the tears of parting hours—
Fall on the bloom of immortal flowers;
No farewells cradle in distant homes
The voice of friends with alien tones;
Nor coldness freezes the warm heart's breath,
With the silent blight of sudden death;
The winter of death worms not the rose
In the fadeless spring of its "deep repose;"
No cold forgetfulness there—no night—
Where God is the sun of life and light.
Dream ye—of all things rich and fair,
The spirits of light or beauty bear;
Whate'er in earth's arcana springs,
Or fancy fans with rainbow wings,
The pictured thoughts—like gems that lie
In the haunted chambers of imag'ry.
Dream ye—of flowers of perennial bloom,
Varied and bright as the peacock's plume;
Gems all glowing with sunset eyes,
Or the ruby light of eastern skies;

The diamond flash of incrusted waves
That burn like day in the sparry caves;
These cannot shadow the music halls,
Or the golden city's jasper walls—
Where the fountain of living water wells,
And the fulness of Godhead unclouded dwells.
One song of joy their full hearts bear,
One anthem rings through the crystal air—
One master-tone his glory flings,
O'er their golden harps' unbroken strings;
Where the sapphire throne makes heaven's day,
And brightens the depths of infinity;
Where the glory of God pours sevenfold light
There is no sin—no sorrow—no night—
Would ye wave their palm of high renown,
"Ye must bear the cross, would you wear the crown."

HEART COMMUNINGS.

"The gush of sacred sympathy,
When heart meets heart in communion sweet,
And the full soul feels what it cannot repeat,
And thought looks out in the speaking eye."

"O! I do love
These low soul communings,—they are to me
The heart's best intercourse." I love to feel
The griefs, the happiness, the unseen wave
Of hearts that give a colour to their life,
Whose streams reflect the light of sacred things,
Hallowed with tones of music from above;
Which, muffled in the veil of secresy,
Finds utterance but in tears, and voiceless prayer.
Whose silent wave ne'er murmurs to the crowd,
Until some friendly hand, with gentle touch,
Unsealed the spring that closed them up with heaven.
Bland sympathy unlocks the sluice of tears—
A channel digs for sorrow's softer flow;
The pent-up flood poured in a kindred heart,
Divided—breaks the burden of the stream,
Whose waters deep had else come o'er the soul,
Rending the clay wall, whose weak strength had sunk
When it looked on the troubled sea of life,—

And fainting faith, saw but the starless night,
Heard but the lashings of the angry deep,
Until he sought again the eye of love;
The star of hope, that guides the foundering bark
Of sea-beat mariner—and felt the hand
Uphold the goings of his faithless feet,
And heard the voice that bids him walk the wave.
When tears gush out to seek a sister tear,
Then sorrow spreads her flood in mingled flow,
The breaking tide imprisoned flows in song,
O'erleaps the rocks, and seeks the "pastures green."
As iron sharpeneth and tempers iron,
So doth the bright'ning face of friend with friend,
When mutual converse polishes the thought,
And eye meets eye, in dewy tenderness.
How the affections warm when heart meets heart,
When word on word doth edge the quick'ning steel
Of "counsel sweet," and pours the precious oil
Of gentle admonition, mind with mind,
In reflex knowledge blending thought of kind,
While in twin moulds their souls, recast by love,
Image the impress of a purer faith.

FAITH, HOPE, LOVE.

"These three."

Thou art a mighty victor, conquering Faith!
  Thy triumphs wear enduring crowns on high;
Thy sons have looked on many-featured death—
  On fire and flood—with calm, unquailing eye.
Up through the golden portals of the sky,
  The fiery chariot o'er the grave has driven,
They flung their mantle down to those who lie
  Low in the dust; whose witness is in heaven,
  Who in the spirit-war have nobly fought and striven.

Hope is a spirit-healer, pouring balm
  On the torn heart, as dew on drooping flowers;
Through the night-watches, with a sleepless calm,
  Cheating death's winter of its chilling powers;
Lighting her silver lamp when gold-day lours;
  Green on the heart, when life's rose-leaves are fading,
Sowing heart's-ease, the seed of fruitage hours,
  When nature's bloom the snowy shroud is shading,
  Life to the weary and the heavy laden.

But thou art strong as death, o'ermastering love,
Clasping soul-links his cold hand cannot break,
Purpling with life, whose deep spring is above,
The veins of feeling flowing through the heart;
Whose streams of sympathy out-gushing, start
To meet the sister-spirit of a friend,
And founts of holy joy and peace impart,
Bonds where the unity of spirit blend,
Whose fruit an incense perfumed heaven-ward send.

Thou hast the world's grey archives richly filled
With deeds of high emprise, and covenants strong;
The life-blush on the face of beauty chilled,
By sacrifice, endurance, deep and long;
Thou art the soul of many a prison song,
Rich offering, costly ransom, life for life,
High sacrifices of heart-martyrdom;
Pouring libations of the passion-strife
On thy high altar, reckless of the knife.

Thou, souls hast interwoven, knit as one
Love, passing that of woman. What so strong?
What hath its tireless ardency not won?
Such David's love to loving Jonathan.
The silver cord is snapt—the music gone,
As the hushed harmony of broken lyre;
The lingering cord then finds no answering tone,
When reft of that which stirred its soul of fire;
But heaven-wedded souls, your love can never tire.

What are the selfish loves, deriving birth
From worldly hearts—the loves of Greece or Rome,
Whose wars have sacked the cities of the earth,
And pillared trophies on the ruined home?
What Damon's love to that of Jonathan
For his soul-wedded David ? knit and twined
Heart within heart, each treasured as his own,
Clasped by the soul-born laws of blending mind,
That closer than sworn covenants can bind.

Death freezes mingling streams of earthly joy,
And creeps like canker o'er the rose's bloom;
The golden bowl, when brimmed without alloy,
Even from our lip is dashed into the tomb;
And such, O! David, was thy friendship's doom,
When dimmed the light of mingling heart-burnings;
When war had sealed the doating soul in gloom,
And broke the chain of sympathetic yearnings,
Thus from thy troubled spirit burst these mournings:

"O! clothe yourselves in sackcloth, Israel's daughters,
For Israel's beauty on high places slain!
Now let your tears o'erflow like gushing waters—
How are the mighty fallen! Saul is slain!
Who'll garnish you in scarlet robes again,
With ornature of gold and rich array;
Weep for the Lord's anointed! on the plain
His shield ingloriously is cast away
As he had ne'er been crowned with majesty!

"O! tell it not in Gath—be this forgot—
For then Philistia's daughters would rejoice!
In streets of Askelon, O! tell it not;
For then the uncircumcised would lift their voice,
And o'er the mighty fallen make a noise.
Strong as the lion, as the eagle fleet,
The warrior bird, that near the sun doth poise
Its dauntless wing; yea, in the battle's heat,
The alien arrows fell around your feet.

"Lovely ye were, as sire and son, in life,
As bud and bough—one in his kingly pride,
A regal branch, and he a blossom rife,
The beautiful! in blood, now side by side.
The spoiler in your death could not divide,
The mingled stream of human hope and fear,
The rushing spirit froze the sunny tide;
My brother, Jonathan! to me so dear,
Now cold and silent on a gory bier!

"How are the mighty fallen! wo is me!
Who now shall strengthen me with counsel sweet?
Thou wert a shield and buckler unto me—
Who in the wilderness the vow repeat,
And gird my heart and hand with promise meet,
And woo my soul to joy in covenant love;
Yea, peril crown and life with me to weep?
Thy love to me was wonderful, above
The love of woman—gentle, strong, and deep!"

LINES ON THE DEATH OF THE REV. DR. MACKINLAY.

"Blessed are the dead who die in the Lord."—Rev. xiv. 13.

SERVANT of God!—thy warfare's o'er—well done!
Now wear the crown of bliss supreme for aye;
The strife is o'er—the glorious victory won!
A dimless star, though systems, suns decay,
Thy soul shall shine through endless, eveless day!
No more thy hand shall aid the poor opprest—
"Allure to brighter worlds—and lead the way;"
Or pour the balm into the wounded breast:
Thy work is done, and thou has entered into rest.

Vicegerent of the Cross!—In battle strong
To wield the spirit-sword and buffet sin—
On Zion's tower a faithful watcher long;
No more thou'lt teach the soul her lamp to trim,
When waning life's faint taper flickers dim;
Or fledge it on the wings of faith to fly,
Or point from Pisgah's top to Jordan's brim—
And clear the lens of faith, for hope's weak eye
To gaze where Canaan blooms with flowers that never die.

No more thou, Patriarch Shepherd, lead'st thy flock
To living waters—as the prophet led
The desert-pilgrims to the stricken rock;
Nor feed'st them—as on Etham's plain he fed
With manna-showers of consecrated bread,
And nursed, with richest dew, his chosen vine.
Thy works will follow,—blessed are the dead
Who sleep in Jesus;—conquering death and time,
They, as the noontide sun, in glory ever shine.

The many weeping hearts that mourn for thee
Embalm thy living memory with tears—
And thou art better from this cloud-land free,
Where being's ageless rose no autumn seres,
But fadeless garlands crown thy fruitful years,
Where Sharon's Rose exhales eternal bloom;
Bearing a seven-fold weight of golden ears,
Thy shock of corn fell ripe into the tomb;
And God's pure lamp has lit death's shadowy gloom.

THE MAN OF SORROWS.

"And they led him away to be crucified, bearing his cross."

Who is He that purple wearing,
All the taunts of malice bearing—
  Silent 'neath the mocker's scorn;
As a lamb to slaughter leading,
Bound and wounded, faint and bleeding,
  Pale and weary—sorrow-worn;
Scourged and smitten, uncomplaining,
Dust and gore his garments staining—
  See! they pierce with thorns his brow;
Fainting, 'neath the cross now bending,
Tears with Salem's daughters blending?
  "Son of Man! 'tis Thou! 'tis Thou."

Hear our sins round Calvary crying,
"Crucify him! crucify him!"
  See! they smite him on the head.
"King of Jews" they, mocking, hail him,
Naked to the tree they nail him,
  'Neath our hands the sinless bled.
Rugged nails his hands have riven,
Hung ashamed 'twixt earth and heaven—

Blameless, numbered with the worst.
O'er his pale face gore-drops streaming,
Frownless still, with love still beaming,
'Neath the wrath of God accurst.

Hark! he prays, while agonizing,
For the murderers who despise him!
Sinners! whence that anguished cry?
"Sore reproach my heart is breaking,
My God! my God! hast Thou forsaken
Thy Beloved—why? oh! why?"
Sin alone could thus accuse him,
Though it pleased the Lord to bruise him,
All our sins were on him laid;
For transgression was he stricken,
For "the sheep the shepherd smitten,"—
Thus the full atonement made.

"It is finished!" hear him crying—
Meekly bows his head, and dying,
Thus He justice satisfies;
With His blood each promise sealing,
Wondrous love to man revealing,
God his covenant ratifies.
Trembling nature quails in thunder,
Heaven, ashamed, grows black with wonder:
See! the sun hath veiled his face!
Hear the awe-struck heathen crying,
"Is the God of nature dying?"
Hath the Eternal left his place?

Heaven and hell around are pressing,
Man's eternal curse or blessing,
  Dead—the Lord of Life to see.
Helpless as an infant sleeping,
Friends—how few! around him weeping,
  Loose him from the bloody tree;
Weeping women o'er him bending,
Trembling fear their bosoms rending,
  Mourn the eclipse of Glory's sun;
While in linen cloths they wind him,
With the cords of death they bind him—
  Can these hold the "Holy One?"

Arch-Apostate! though you slay him,
In the dust of death you lay him,
  Thou hast bruised his heel at length!
See his garments! O! how glorious!
Travelling in his might victorious—
  Edom! He hath spoiled thy strength.
Father—God! oh! what could move him,
"Sons of Adam" thus to love them,
  Thus to give the Son to death?
'Tis His will, and thou hast done it,
Take "the kingdom, thou hast won it,
  Even so," the Father saith.

Salem—see thy waning glory,
Clouds of doom are gathering o'er thee—
  Now thy fallen shrine grows dark;

Stars on Zion-hill declining,
Tell the promised Sun is shining!
  Hark! they echo—" we depart."
See, the Temple vail is rending!
See, the rising God ascending!
  "King of Glory enter in."
Thou the gates of brass hast riven,
Paved a way from earth to heaven—
  Pardon's won for darkest sin.

To the inner shrine returning,
With unceasing incense burning,
  Blood-bought mercy to proclaim;
Lift the sceptre, reign for ever—
Worthy is the Lamb for ever—
  Worthy is the Lamb once slain.
Sacrifice, by God appointed,
Rich with gifts for men anointed,
  Shadows melt in perfect day;
Prophet, Priest, and Mediator,
Man-Redeemer, God, Creator—
  Aaron cast thy robes away.

Christ is mighty to deliver,
Mercy is built up for ever
  In the broken law fulfilled;
His own right hand the curse removed,
God well pleased in the Beloved—
  Sinai's peals in Calvary stilled.

In the great propitiation,
Sin condemned, proclaim salvation,
  Sinner, here your "sentence" see.
See the debt your sins had spotted,
By his Holy arm there blotted,
  Nailed upon the accursed tree.

See the cleansing "fountain open,"
In his body bruised and broken,
  Pardon through atoning blood;
Righteousness by faith revealing,
Here for every wound is healing,
  Peace proclaimed 'twixt man and God.

EVER WITH THEE.

"And so we shall ever be with the Lord."

EVER with Thee! with thee for ever, ever;
Rest in thy love without a fear of change;
No night, no thought of sin, to make us sever—
No foe, our hearts' affections to estrange.

Ever with Thee! amid ten thousand chiefest,
Beholding in my heart beside thee none;
Whilst thou thy endless tale of love repeatest,
Gaze on thy face, and see thee only—ONE.

Ever with Thee! where all the lovely gather,
Forgetting all their loves, to sing of thine;
Dwell in thy love, the bosom of the Father,
Filled with thy beauty—thine while thou art mine.

Ever with Thee! where breathes no thought of grieving,
Where sighing shall for ever pass away:
Where falls no tear—where pains no heart deceiving;
Where comes no death—no shadow of decay!

Ever with Thee! where burns no thought of parting—
No longing yearnings—where no absence pains—
There's from the "many mansions" no departing;
One family, where love in glory reigns.

Ever with Thee, filled with a joy unbounded,
What, in the fulness of that joy, may be
Nearest the throne, by seraphim surrounded,
In everlasting songs still praising Thee.

LOVE.

"There is a love that cannot die"

THERE is a love that's pure—pure as the mountain snows,
There is a love that fades swift as a blighted rose,
There is a love that's true as magnet to the pole,
There is a love that clings like body to the soul,
There is a love that lives deep—deep within the heart,
There is a love that stings, aye, like a poisoned dart,
There is a love whose ties, nor time, nor death can sever,
A love whose home is in the skies—it lives and lives for ever.

GLEANINGS OF PROPHECY.

I.—RETURNING ISRAEL.

UP, up to Jerusalem, the darkness is breaking
That long has beclouded lost Israel's light;
The daughter of Judah from slumbers awaking,
The morning star chasing the shadows of night.

The Spirit of God, in the valley of vision,
Is breathing and shaking the dry parched bones;
They mourn, who at Calvary laughed in derision—
Jerusalem is precious, though scattered her stones.

The long-cherished olive, though barren and blighted,
By lightnings from heaven, on Solyma's plain;
The dews that once fed on its branches have lighted—
The glory of Leb'non is budding again.

Put on thy rich garment, O daughter of Zion!
Nor weep on the ruin of Salem's high towers;
The Lamb to green pastures, not Judah's wroth Lion,
Is wooing thee back to thy desolate bowers.

Take thy harp from the willows and strike it again,
Let the songs of loved Zion deliverance bring;
The olive is spreading on Jordan's green plain—
Of the beauty of Carmel, oh, Israel sing!

O! cast off her sackcloth, and shake off her dust,
  Bind the wounds of the chosen, still dripping with gore;
Let the sword that has smitten against her, now rust,
  And with darkest judgments, O pierce her no more!

Her waters are bitter, she murmuring grieves,
  But the Branch of the Promise with fragrance still teems;
O! cast in the branch with its sweetening leaves,
  Till Isael's wanderers drink of the streams.

Though bleeding with stripes, all landless and homeless,
  The pilgrim to Canaan for refuge still looks;
Let those streams from the stricken rock gladden their loneness,
  Like springs in the desert, and trees by the brooks.

As dew-drops on Hermon, the promised seed gathers,
  To hail the arising of Righteousness' Sun;
The morning of beauty foretold by the fathers—
  The set time to favour loved Zion is come.

The God of their fathers remembers them still,
  And nations in darkness shall spring into birth,
When the Spirit-Shekinah relumes Zion hill,
  And a halo of glory illumines the earth.

He shall visit the vine that from Egypt he brought,
  To plant by the Jordan on Jericho's plains;
'Twill wither no more with the wilderness drought—
  He'll water its boughs with the latter-day rains.

To nourish its verdure He'll cast out the heathen,
Till as cedars in Leb'non it spreadeth its roots,
And feed with rich dews, as He fed it on Etham,
Till from sea to river its broad shadow shoots.

Then the waste, as the garden of Eden, shall bloom,
The fair Rose of Sharon its glory there shed;
The fragrance of Leb'non the valleys perfume—
The olive and lily their beauty there spread.

Go up to Jerusalem, rebuild Salem's shrine,
Cry aloud, that the days of her mourning may cease;
Let your feet on the mountains of Israel shine,
How beautiful those who bring tidings of peace!

Go, point to "the blue wave of deep Galilee,"
Where o'er its foam-billow Immanuel trod,
When he stilled, with a word, the wild wrath of the sea,
And draw them, while sinking, to her risen God.

II.—ISRAEL, A BUD OF PROMISE.

"Israel shall blossom and bud, and fill the face of the world with fruit."
ISAIAH xxvii. 6.

THERE is promise in a bud,
While its heart is yet unsealed,
Ere life-hues flush, with stirring blood,
The glories of the summer wood,
As the olive branch waved o'er the flood,
In folded leaves concealed.

There is hope in opening leaves,
As timidly they peep,
And the bursting bud its breast upheaves
With wealth of future golden eves;
For earth her wreath of promise weaves,
While tears her blossoms steep.

There is joy in bright green leaves,
While they look out for the sun
From the shadows of the morning cloud,
Till the festal song of earth is loud,
And day-spring rend the wintry shroud
Of nature dark and dim.

There is a prayer in soft leaves,
While they whisper o'er the earth—
The worship of the leafy hours,
The song of praise amid the flowers;
'Tis the incense-breath of blossom showers
Singing o'er autumn's birth.

Buds on a fallen tree,
Though peeled in branch and root,
Its leafy honours trampled low,
A sapless, bent, and broken bough,
May, when the enliv'ning waters flow,
To palmy beauty shoot.

Fair, from the ancient stem
  Of Israel, there has grown
A glorious Branch, whose trampled root
A swaying rod o'er earth shall shoot;
Earth's gathering tribes shall seek His fruit
  With Israel, His own.

As a teil tree, or an oak—
  The life hid in its heart—
Though over earth its leaves be cast;
Borne far, and torn by every blast;
With holy seed unfolds, at last,
  Its fruit shall ne'er depart.

That once green olive tree,
  Fostering our alien bough—
The native branches cast away,
Ingraffed again—no sin-decay
Shall blight, till in a glorious day
  Its seed to fruitage grow.

Their rod is in your hand,
  As Aaron's sapless rod,
A pleader for the captive band;
Life from the dead, at your command,
To bud and blossom will expand,
  Fanned by the breath of God.

Still bow on Carmel's top,
  As the prophet knelt of old;
Look toward the sea, nor cry "Alas!
I nothing see, the heavens are brass;"
Still plead till seven times shall pass—
  The little cloud behold.

It saith, "The Lord is God,"
  By Israel's broken shrine,
Amid the blood of prophets slain
Their hearts return to him again—
The drooping sound of latter rain
  Doth visit *now* his vine.

III.—CHRIST WEEPING OVER JERUSALEM.

"Jesus wept."

'Twas eve in Palestine!—departing day
  Slept calmly on the lake of Galilee;
To vermil shadows crept the purple ray,
  A smoking cloud loomed o'er "Sodoma's sea;"
Green Tabor rose in hoar sublimity—
  Dim Moab stretched afar in fading light—
The palmy Jordan rolled on silently—
  The vine breathed balm on Carmel's flowery height,
  On Hermon fell the tears of coming night.

In regal glory, like an eastern queen,
  In robe of wreathed gold and precious stone,
Pillar on pillar, glassed in marble sheen,
  Jerusalem sat upon her mountain throne;
High tower o'er tower, like Alpine glaciers shone,
  Mocking the Syrian heaven with amber glow;
Fair, on Moriah's brow, a golden crown,
  Her temple pinnacles, like rose-dyed snow,
  Smiled o'er the pools and olive vales below.

On Olive's brow there stood a weary man,
Gazing on Zion's glory and her pride,
Fast tear on tear adown his pale cheek ran—
  Why did he weep? The anthem scarce had died
That hailed him King of Salem—still the tide
  Of triumph lingered on the temple-way,
Fainting afar on Calvary's rocky side,
  Its echoing wave ebbed with the dying day,
  Where praise her garments spread still green the palm-branch lay.

Creation's heart so moved, that all can move!
  The fulness of His passion to express,
Big with the tender pain of slighted love—
  Throbbing to anguish 'neath the menial dress
  Of feeble flesh. Love-shrouded loveliness!
Why breaks thy soul with melting tenderness?
  The meek, the beautiful, the undefiled!
Embodied pity! kind in thy distress;
  So strong, so gentle, beautifully mild;
The God-man weeping as a weaned child!

Do prophet shadows crimson now the tear,
  Purpling thy passion-flowers, Gethsemane?
Fainting beside the brook, with wildering fear,
  Feels he, in thought, the sweat of agony?
Has Calvary's gory picture filled his eye?
  Ah! stricken deer, by archers sorely prest,
Emptied of all save love, he weltering lay,
  Wrath's arrows drinking dry his spirit's rest,
  Wringing, with griefs untold, his troubled breast.

Blood-dewed Gethsemane! love-hallowed spot!
  Calm as a temple sleeps thy olive shade;
E'en Calvary's altar-fires seem now forgot,
  Beyond green Bethany His eye has strayed,
Where friendship ne'er forsook and ne'er betrayed—
  Where sympathy, ineffably benign,
Out-welled through chinks His soul-revealings made,
  Unveiled the glories of the inner shrine,
  So spiritually fair the guest Divine!

Not to condemn thee—Shiloh sent to bless!
  Oft mercy's golden pitcher He did fill,
Poured out his soul in words of tenderness,
  Wand'ring all soft as Siloe's shady rill,
In streams of gentleness round Zion hill,
  In one surcharging fount his heart o'erflowed.
Hear how it bleeds, and yearns o'er Salem still,
  While through his higher nature purely glowed
  The exquisite compassions of our God!

"As the hen shades her brood I'd gather thee,
Jerusalem! O Jerusalem! even thou!
Why would ye die? ye will not come to me,
My prophets' blood o'erveils thy guilty brow;
How shall I give thee up, O Ephraim! how?
In this thy day 'my peace' if thou hadst known;
O'er thee compassion's wing is folding now,
I see thy tribes far from their fallen throne,
Thy house all desolate, thine ephod gone!"

To Tophet's edge with tears he followed thee,
Lost on the shore of heaven, a castaway
On mercy's verge; day on thy shoreless sea
Closes her weeping eye, which love's long ray
Stretched to the acme of thy destiny;
The deluge-wave bears on the passing ark,
Like life's last gleam in death's extremity;
His eye Divine affects his human heart,
Sees on Salvation's Rock a wreck thy spirit-barque.

'Tis night in Palestine. Now brimmed with doom,
A cup of mixture red is in her hands;
Soon she must drink. Round her Pretorium loom
The Gentile spear. Truth, 'mid Rome's legion-bands,
Near a stained pillar, mute as marble stands,
With face serenely pale—a wounded form;
Judah her God with stripes and insult brands;
She wreathes for empires' King a *crown of thorn*,
Toiling and bleeding up the hill of scorn.

If wrath *so* burn that Plant of heavenly bloom,
  If in this fair *green* tree such things be done,
If judgment-fires, unwithered, so consume
  "The Righteous Branch"—so scorch that Holy One;
If sin condemn, so bruise, the Anointed One—
  The Bud of Prophecy's unfolding flower—
What shall be done, when He so pierced shall come,
  In branches *dry*, who flout His thunder's power,
  When breaks *this* bough beneath the fiery shower?

'Tis night in Palestine? Jerusalem banned!
  God's judgments and His word *has* come to pass;
"A heap of witness" is her wasted land,
  Now Ephraim's crown is withered as the grass;
'Mid her foundations strangers cry, "Alas!"
  And on Mount Zion ploughed in dust, they say,
"O Ichabod!" destruction's burning lash
  Has marred her beauty in the cloudy day,
  Her gates are all forsaken utterly!

IV.—"SHEAR JASHUB." *

A VOICE is heard in Ramah—bitter weeping—
  Lone Rachel wailing for her trampled dead;
And tears in bitterness her soul is steeping,
  And dust is thrown upon her lovely head.

* The remnant shall return.

Ah! sackcloth as a cloud is o'er her spread,
All comfortless she wrings her folded hands,
Because her loved ones are not;—they have led
Her children captive into stranger lands,
And torn and broken all their joyous bands.

Her Eden-land is now a desolation!
The glory of all lands a desert plain;
And peeled, and scattered over every nation,
A by-word and a hissing is her name.
She hath no prince, no sacrifice, no fane;
The sword has ploughed her vineyard as a flood;
Her priests, her mighty men of war, are slain,
They shroudless lie in Hinnom in their blood—
The palmer-worm has nipt the olive bud.

Why is the queen of cities sitting solitary,
Clothed as a widow, in the dust, alone!
Weeping because of her idolatry,—
Lovers who called her beautiful are gone,
And of her many people there are none—
No echoing sound on her weed-matted streets—
In dwellings desolate, no voice of song;
And of her daughters fair, no dancing feet
In mirthful echoes to the timbrel beat.

She that exalted was above the stars,
Why is her glorious beauty cast from heaven?
The tear upon her cheek her beauty mars—
Why is her rich embroidered garment riven?

God, as an enemy, has with her striven,
  Her faithless children into Egypt sold;
Baptized "Lo-ammi" to the desert driven,
  An "outcast," wandering from the pasture fold,
  Because she bowed unto the calf of gold.

And this is Zion, whom no one seeks after;
  A valley filled with bones, exceeding dry;
Where the avenging sword was sheathed in slaughter—
  Priests of the living God ! O prophecy !
Comfort ye, comfort ye, Jerusalem ! cry ;—
  O Spirit ! breathe upon these many slain—
On these long desolations cast thine eye—
  Bring Israel's hope out of the grave again !
  Thy people chosen—called by thy name.

THE MARTYRS' GRAVES.

GRATEFULLY INSCRIBED TO THE REV. R. SIMPSON, AUTHOR OF "TRADITIONS OF THE COVENANTERS," &C., &C.

"When your children shall ask their fathers in time to come, saying, 'What *mean* these stones?' then ye shall let your children know."—JOSHUA iv. 21, 22.

"Thy martyr kirk! O! Scotland!
Strong as our mountain oak,
The deeper shaken by the storm,
The firmer clasped the rock;
The winds may bear its shady leaves
Far over field and flood,
But its roots are in our country's heart,
And watered with her blood."

O! MARTYR-SPRINKLED Scotland!
Thy covenanted dust,
Like gold amid our mountains,
Gleam through tradition's rust.
We bless the hands that tear away
Dark weeds from martyr graves,
And graving o'er time's mossy urns,
Faith's witness story saves.
Thy *auld grey stones* are sprinkled with
"Blood poured like water free,"
And speak in holy oracles,
O! martyr-land to thee.
These altar stones of sacrifice,
Incarnate truth hath stored,
Where faith, in love-drawn characters,
Her red libation poured.

Like promise-stars in heaven's eye,
The lyart and the leal,
Sleep lonely by the heath-bound tarn,
Where eerie cries the teal.
Their prophet-mantles rolled in blood,
By tribulation riven,
From Scotland's ark drove back the flood,
"That chased them up to heaven;"
Where Peden bold, in flood and fold,
On mountain, moor, or glen,
All seer-like, bore salvation's cup
To fainting martyr-men;
When heaven's brooding wing of love,
Like Israel's pillar-cloud,
Them lapped in nature's misty tent,
A prayer-woven shroud.
Their home was oft the mountain cave,
Their couch the waving fern,
Their pillow oft the grey-moss stone,
In moorlands dark and stern.
'Mid bleatings of the mountain lamb,
The melody of rills,
The moss-hag, 'mid the purple blooms,
Deep in the heathy hills;
The auld cairn, where the plover wails,
And fern and thistle waves,
'Mid green spots in the wilderness—
There seek the martyrs' graves.

PILGRIM SKETCHES.

I.—THE VISION OF PROPHECY.

O LOVELY Italy! thou art
Like faded works of glorious art—
Still thou art beauteous in decay,
  Although thy colours faded lie—
All dim with dust—in ruin grey—
  Once rich and varied as thy sky.
The outline may alone remain
  Of former beauty,—still we gaze
Enwrapt upon the tarnished frame—
  The mighty shade of ancient days—
Engraven with the high in name,
Who gilt thy land with deathless fame.
Though beauty was thy costly dower,
  And flung her tissue over thee,
Thou wert a monster—in thy power
  Dreadful and strong exceedingly—
Such as the heaven-inspired seer *
Saw in prophetic vision clear.

* Dan. vii. 7.

The world's trembling empire cowered
  Beneath thy wide extended jaws—
That oft with iron teeth devoured,
  And reckless tore with brazen claws
  The empires of the earth apart,
And held beneath thy lion-paws
  The prostrate world's fast heaving heart.
Thou brok'st in pieces sceptres, thrones—
  And trampled kingdoms 'neath thy feet,
Regardless of thy captives' groans,
  Until thy measure was complete—
And full of conquest, crime, and blood,
It overwhelmed thee like a flood.

II.—THE POWER AND GLORY OF ROME.

Rome sat in mountain majesty
  Upon her high imperial throne;
Circled with martial pageantry,
  Proud, peerless, great, alone.
Her footstool was the neck of kings—
  Her lofty throne the conquered earth;
And still the kneeling nations sing
  Of mighty Rome's immortal birth!
"Baptized eternal!"—and arrayed
  In gold and purple—"Queen of Nations!"
She deemed her marble pillars laid
  Immovable as earth's foundations.

Where'er her conquering eagle flew,
  Monarchs became her bleeding prey;
Their sceptres at her feet they threw,
  And bowed beneath her potent sway;
Where'er her banner was unfurled,
They owned her mistress of the world!
Till when arose the little horn,*
By which her kingdoms were uptorn;
The sceptred hand, the mitred head,
That kings and kingdoms captive led;
Whose dictatorial voice could sway
Proud senates—whose imperious nod
The millions trembled to obey,
And hailed her pontiff—demi-god!
Whose will, like to a mighty soul,
Could bridle by unseen control,
Or move the ruling powers of earth,
And give to sleeping nations birth;
Who held the reins of every state—
In court, in camp, and cabinet.

III.—THE FALL OF ROME.

In dust and sackloth—widowed now,
  "The nursing mother of young nations,"
With wrinkles on her crownless brow,
  The ravages of Time's mutations,

* Revelations xvii. 8.

Sits on the tomb of fallen state,
In sorrow, lone, and desolate.
Her temples crumble in decay—
Her mighty Cæsars—where are they?
Her soaring eagles?—ever fled;
Her tribunes? —mingled with the dead;
Her forum—where her Tully thundered?—
Amid colossal ruins numbered;
And Ichabod in palace halls
Is written on their broken walls.
'Twas in the zenith of her power
  The fulness of her glory died;
Then, fell dark retribution's hour,
  The Martyr's blood for vengeance cried,
And Judgment drew her glittering sword,
  And from the mountain cut the stone
That, rolled on by the savage horde,
  Soon broke her adamantine throne.
Like torrents from their German source,
  A flood of Goths and Vandals rushed,
And with a dread impetuous force,
  Like bursting waters, wildly gushed;
That living stream of salient life
  Far spreading, desolation dark,
Roused her, while sleeping, into strife,
  And, rushing on her mighty heart,
Benumbed her energies, and laid
  The great Goliah in the dust—
And ruin o'er him flung her shade,
  And hung his armour up to rust.

IV.—THE COLISEUM.

Colossal ruin! child of man!
  Huge nursling of his pride and power,
Where Time's transforming talisman
  Has glassed the shade of glory's hour.
What read we—on thy mountain walls,
  Plaything of kingdoms rent and riven?
Lone echo 'mid thy ruin calls,
  Whose Babel pillars flout the heaven;—
Whence all this pomp of trophied gloom
  O'er empires' giant skeleton?—
This mockery, on glory's tomb;
  This sculpture on the grave of Rome?
Here read her epitaph and doom;
The worm that writhed 'neath Cæsar's wheel,
  Has thrashed this mountain in his wrath;
Yea, gnawed with rust her arm of steel,
  And strewed with wrecks his thunder path,
When Faith became a nation's play,
  Her warrior kings a Nero's mirth,
A plaything to the beasts of prey,
  And stained with crime the Roman earth;
Their blood, which crieth from the dust,
  Then wrote deep curses on thy brow—
Which eats with retribution's rust,
  The sceptre of thy kingdom now.
Still in these awful ruins frown
  The curse that broke thy empire's horn,
Which dimmed the rays of Cæsar's crown,
  That moth hath Rome's purple torn.

Now Art again to Nature swells—
That mountain, cloven into dells,
  Like toppling precipice and glade,
Where lawny spots of scattered green,
  'Neath forest peaks of Alpine shade,
'Mid heaps of shattered arches gleam;
  Where arch o'er arch in thousands rise,
In circles after circle run,
  Like mountain cliffs that ape the skies,
And wrap in twilight-gloom the sun.
Vast crags and shattered fragments torn,
  Jut each o'er each, in giddy height—
Broken, and rifted by the storm;
  Bathing their brows in purple light,
Whose rifted stones terrific frown!
  High walls o'er walls in mountain might
  The zenith pierce, till reels the sight,
Where the blue heavens roll liquid down,
  Like moonbeams through the clouds of night.
Through windows vast by time o'erworn,
  The low winds, gushing, weep and sigh,
Like mournful strains of Æolia born,—
  A soft and plaintive minstrelsy—
Where Nature's fitful requiems mourn,
  That aught so like her own could die;
Her fingers robe thy naked form
  And wreathe of weeds a crown for thee;
Thou'rt kingly still, though dust deform
  Thy bald head's crownless majesty;
  The gold of the Italian sky

Through myrtle-trellised pillars stream,
To where weed-matted fragments lie,
Like temples in an Eastern dream,
Of capital and canopy.
Where marble-rooted fig-tree weaves,
Of blossomed boughs, a dark arcade,
Of tangled weeds and feathery leaves,
O'er rifted roofs, a cypress shade;
And strange flowers with their meek eyes smile,
And cling around the giant pile;
And velvet moss-tufts' silken green,
And dark grass, like dishevelled hair,
Droops purple—sculptured piles between;
And younglings of the forest there
The vaulted roofs and arches bear.
The olive wild, and wreathy vine,
The balmy snow-flowered jessamine;
The bramble and the soft bright grass
Curtain the fallen capital,
And trickling sounds of water pass
Where crevice-gathered rain-drops fall;
Faint sounds—like fountains in a wood,
Stirring its leafy solitude;
And rustlings of the wild dove's wing,
While from their mossy nest they spring,
Cooped in the sculpture deep and grey,
Of some vast pillar's tracery,
Where Art its wealth of name had wrought,
And robed the rugged stone in thought.

Now, there decay's corroding breath
  Is gnawing on its marble strength,
Where worm and weed, the kin of death,
  Are trailing o'er its prostrate length;
Whose marble sheen has glossed the rays
  Of gleamig spear and jewelled crown,
When trident and the altar's blaze
  Drew Rome's imperial thunders down.
The monuments ambition rears,
  The palace, dome, and temple, rust;
The name which grew above its peers,
The flood of Time, like waters, wears
  To sand its rock-built trust;
The tomb, though washed by thousand tears,
  Where glory graves her name,
Grows dim beneath the rush of years;
Her teeth the battle banner tears,
And tottering age no longer hears
  Her trumpet sounding name.
And thus these air-built temples fall,
  Earth's glory gilded clay.
Wealth, honour, pleasure, passion, all,
Death, dust, and darkness cover shall,
Till wrapt in Time's oblivious pall,
  Like dreams—they pass away!

LINES,

ON A MONUMENT TO THE MEMORY OF CAPTAIN WILSON OF THE BENGAL NATIVE INFANTRY, WHO FELL IN THE ACTION OF THE KYBER PASS; EXECUTED BY THAT EMINENT SCULPTOR, FILLANS OF LONDON.

"The sculptor, painter, an' the bard."

"Beauteous exceedingly, each polished line,
Of chiseled poetry! where master mind,
His high conceptions of proportion fine,
In marble portraiture has well defined;
Embodying, in cold and frozen stone,
The breathing thought, those rich creations rife,
With stirring soul, of such expressive tone,
'As warms the marble with pathetic life;'
Stamping upon each image cold and fair,
Passions subdued, or anguish-breathing air."

SAY, warrior-band, why drop the spear
At the feet of the fallen brave?
Why bear him away on a musket bier,
To dig him a lonely grave?
Why must he sleep, his march now o'er,
'Neath some memorial stone?
Why not, 'mong garments rolled in gore,
In the battle-mound unknown?
The dweller gone, let the fallen tent
On the red field trampled lie;
Nay, for the *good*, or his mantle rent,
"Even *some* would dare to die."

One kneels, that his drooping brow may rest,
  Unawed 'mid the battle's thunder;
Their swords the tent 'round his dreamless breast,
  To shield from the alien's plunder.
Another turns, with wistful eye,
  A thought of tears to smother,
As if he'd lay his banner by,
  And bear his warrior brother.
'Tis the marble speaks! and a mournful tale
  This silent stone is telling,
Of carnage dark, in an Indian vale,
  And the soldier's lonely dwelling.
Here love embalms the honoured dead,
  Beyond the deep now lying,
Till the voiceless group, in solemn tread,
  Move slow o'er "the dead and dying"
They live in the sculptor-poet's thought,
  Which awes the soul to wonder,
By the plastic hand of genius brought,
  'Neath the loom of the battle thunder.
How strange, yet true, this cold white stone,
  So still and soulless sleeping,
Through the chiselled picture lines alone,
  Can brim our hearts to weeping;
'Tis the poet-soul that burns and breathes,
  In each hieroglyphic word,
That twines her monumental wreaths
  Around his lyre and sword.

THE PASTOR'S WELCOME.

Spirit of Truth! descend, with dove-like wing,
In plenteous unction, on that chosen head;
The golden urn of light supernal bring,
And oil of grace, in gifts of *blessing* shed;
O'er him salvation, as a garment, spread—
A prophet-mantle of love-missioned zeal—
That he the courts of praise with *peace* may tread,
And we heart-ministrations *daily* feel,
In *truth*, as dews of consolation steal.

Pure, from the altar of consummate love,
A vessel, fitted glorious things to bear;
Fire, burning from the inner shrine above,
The fulness of *His* counsel to declare:
May we uphold his trusting hands in prayer,
While he uplifts, o'er floods, the promise rod,
And breathes on fainting souls Edenic air,
In strength of him who paths of trial trod—
Girt as a holy teacher come from God.

Watchman! irradiant on the tower of faith,
Hold up thy torch against the midnight sky,—
Awake the dreamer from the sleep of death—
O! point to judgment, and of mercy cry;
Unfold "the scrolls that teach to live and die,"
Whose words despised, shall turn to flames of fire,
To chase the soul through dark eternity,—
Rivers of "Unregenerating fire,"
Onwards, still onwards, burning ne'er to tire.

What of His night?—its darkness and its power—
The passion-drops of soul-wrung agony—
The wonderment of love's consummate hour—
The rack of nature's deep extremity;
In struggling for the crowning mastery,
Alone the travail of His spirit trod
The wine-press of endurance and dismay,
He quaffed the cup of trembling—grasped the rod,
Pledged on the fast-enduring oath of God.

What of our night?—by angel justice driven
Far from the hill of God—his holy place—
Our sins had barred the golden gates of heaven—
We threw them back in mercy's lovely face.
Watchman! hold up the mystic cross of grace,
The center-poise on which creation hung,
Where righteousness and peace with smiles embrace,
There truth and mercy met, of pardon sung,
Till heaven and earth with joyful tidings rung.

When green mortality, as rose-leaves, fade,
Or grasps the ebbing world with palsied hand,
Beside the floods that wrap the vale of shade,
Do thou, a ministering angel, stand
With shadowed glimpses of "the better land;"
O! cast the rays of hope far in the deep,
When Azriel's sun-darkening wings expand,
And leave pale shadows on the mourner's cheek,
Then, bear the oil of tears to Jesus's feet.

And thus the angel-graces shall descend,
A comely chain to draw the soul on high,
And on the golden links of love ascend,
Whose hand of mediation doth ally
Imperfect dust to perfect Deity—
And binds the earth unto the sapphire throne,
To hold intense communion with the sky;
Where pure, the watcher, as the Holy One,
Is crowned with stars, and vestured with the sun.

The teeming riches of the gifted mind,
Vowed to the temple, on the altar laid.
By sense intern, in high communion shrined
To God thy glory, who a sun and shade,
Shall glorify the thoughts that cannot fade;
As star-fires from the lips of wisdom poured,
To light our moral night, till darkness fade,
And God in all, through all, shall be adored,
On earth as heaven—by "truth's omnific word."

TIME'S WARNING.

AFTER THE MANNER OF "DELTA."

"Say, do the hours, when circling round,
Ne'er strike thy heart with solemn sound."

OLD Father Time! turn up thy glass,
The last sand of the lingering year
Drops in the Abyss we ne'er repass,
Deep-furrowed with the smile and tear.
Thus one by one in darkness drops,
Unnumbered by the careless eye,
The birth-day of eternal hopes—
The hours by which we live and die;
Think!--from this fleeting dream of strife,
We wake but when we die—to life!

How goes the time? What hast thou done?
The night comes on—the shadows haste;
In darkness sinks thy setting sun,
With golden talents run to waste.

Ever! for ever! heart, now hear
The pendulum of unceasing pain—
The wheel of torture's ceaseless tear,
Drop—dropping with its fiery rain,—
The wail of souls in darkness tost—
Time lost! for ever, ever lost!

How goes the time?—Come, answer me?
Grim death cries to the old and young,
Work while 'tis day—I come for thee,
Though time should plead with iron tongue;
Now count thy years—what may they be?
How many lost in Folly's maze?
How many talents stored for me?—
Nay, start not at my solemn face!
How burns thy lamp?—the Master calls—
Thy tale is told—the curtain falls!

How goes the time?—My morn is bright,
My cheek now glows in beauty's bloom;
'Tis long till noon—why speak of night?
No clouds foretell the evening's gloom,—
Hark! Death now whets his glittering scythe,
Nor waits for Time's corroding rust;
A field-flower, soon cut down, it lieth—
A rosebud trampled in the dust,—
The canker 'neath the purple lies,
That glows and brightens while it dies.

How goes the time?—'Tis height of noon,
  Swift as a shade my days decline;
The shadows flee—and soon, too soon,
  Will fall the dial's dark'ning line.
Now, *Wisdom* cries, "All flesh is grass,"
  Its glory as a flower is gone;
The autumn wind doth o'er it pass,
  And of its place no more is known—
The fathers! where, alas, are they?
The prophets! do they live for aye?

How goes the time?—My sand runs low,
  Drop, dropping—soon the last will fall;
My trembling heart, and pulses slow,
  Life's poisoned honey turns to gall.
How went thy time? even as a post,
  O'er-burdened to the judgment day
With crime-rolls of a spirit lost,
  To tell of mercies lost for aye;—
All cloudy, weary, wintry days,
"Evil and few," the patriarch says.

Watchmen, what of the night?—Ho! tell
  Time foots it quick with measured pace—
Ring loud the soul's alarum bell,
  To note how night creeps on apace.
Death knocks—he's waiting at the door;
  Time cries, "Prepare to meet thy God;"

For young, for old, for rich and poor,
  Old Sexton turns the grassy sod,—
Wormed all, earth's greenest shadows fade,
Fleet as the gourd, once Jonah shade.

The angel folds his raven wing,
  The arrow's set, the bow is bent;
For thee or me he draws the string—
  To-day! to-day! repent! repent!
Mute, on thy brow, and lip, and eye,
  To-morrow his pale seal may rest;
Shall angels sing, where cold you lie,
  The weary entered into rest;
Or, wilt thou cry, life's vapour o'er,
"A kingdom! for one moment more!"

A HARVEST HYMN.

PSALM LXV. 13.

LIFT up! lift up the heart in song,
  Lift up the drooping head,
See, on our valleys and our hills
  A bounteous hand out-spread;
The earth, beneath its power, has turned
  Like clay unto the seal,
Where love, in characters of light,
  His attributes reveal,
Who feeds the lion in the wild,
  The ravens when they call,
Who clothes the lilies of the field,
  And notes the sparrow's fall;
Who scattereth his radiant cloud
  In pearls o'er the earth,
And wearieth its murky folds
  To feed the violet's birth;
Like as a tabernacle spreads
  His garment on the sea,
And thunders in the living light,
  In glorious majesty.

The shadowy light of April skies,
That sows her hope in tears,
Has showered with smiles, in nature's lap,
A flood of golden ears;
The golden horn of plenty pours
Her clusters in the vale,
The music of the reapers' song
With gladness fills the gale;
The purple wreath of summer crowns
The hills with living gold,
Where autumn binds her rustling sheaf
With fruits an hundred fold.
O! not a breeze that bears to us
The odour of the rose,
And on the fevered brow of care
In healthful fragrance blows,—
O! not a daisy-cup whereon
Our careless footsteps tread,—
Or twinkling star in night that pours
Its glory on our head,—
O! not a valley-stream that sings
In beauty to the hills,
Where, through the rent of riven rock,
Rejoice the ocean rills,—
Nor bird that fans the amber-cloud,
With iris-coloured wings,
Or, in the whispering shade of woods,
In choral anthem sings,—
Nor bee that bends the honey-cup,
Low harping in the grass,—

No silver atom-flies, that masqued
In dazzling sunbeams pass,—
Nor aught on which "the regent sun"
"Looks from his throne above,"
But lifts its heart in praise to God—
Is eloquent of love.
That love the living element
In which creation swims,
Where wisdom hides her wondrous skill,
Whence earth with goodness teems;
From where the huge leviathan
Plays 'mid the sparry caves,
Where rosy-shells as star-light gleam
Amid the deep blue waves;
Where, 'mid the wreck of empire, sleep
The earth's unshrouded dead,
The wealth of trophied argosies
Have sunk as rain or lead,
To where she flings her gorgeous gems
In pearls at our feet,
And murmurs, like a dreaming child,
In swaddling bands asleep;
From where the pine with verdure plumes
The eagle-cliffs dark crown,
To where the crystal avalanche
On steeps appaling frown;
From India's burning heart of gold,
To Lapland's snowy north,
The green earth, from her million store,
Pours endless treasures forth,

To breath of soft Hesperian climes,
  That fan the orange bowers,
Or odour from the eastern vine
  Where fall the olive flowers;
To where, 'mid gold-commingled sand,
  The wild sirocco's ire,
Digs for the lofty palm a tomb,
  Where sweeps her wing of fire;
Where'er on earth a lily blows,
  Where falls a drop of dew,
In herbless waste where springs a flower,
  It speaks of care for you.
How blind the heart that seeth not
  The veil material riven,
A shadow of the Infinite,
  On the unbounded heaven!
Who hives not wisdom in the heart
  Even from a drop of dew,—
Who sees not heaven reflected
  Even in the wild weeds' hue,—
In the light to love accessible
  High on creation's throne,
There throbs a heart of sympathy
  In music with thine own.
The hand once pierced with rugged nails
  Moves nature's mystic wheels,
And on the circle of event
  His faithfulness reveals;
Where, from the breast of mercy,
  Still soft words of pity glow,

From lips that blanched on Golgotha,
O ! hear what accents flow,—
" O, man ! the seasons shall revolve,
While sun and moon endure,
Thy bread shall still be given thee,
Thy water shall be sure."
He hungered in the wilderness,
In trial, toil, and tears,
Who holds the waters in His hand,
And leads the golden spheres.
Trust, and he shall, o'er darkest seas,
Outstretch the promise-rod—
Lift up your heart in thankfulness,
And praise your Saviour God.

THE LAZARETTO.

In the south of Africa, there is a large lazar-house for lepers. It is enclosed by a very high wall, and has only *one* entrance, which is strictly guarded—no one who enters by that awful gate is ever allowed to return. Within this abode of misery there are multitudes of lepers, in all stages of the disease; but you will ask who cares for the souls of the hapless inmates? who will venture in? who will forsake all to carry the message of a Saviour? Two Moravian missionaries, impelled by a Divine love, have chosen the lazar-house as their field of labour; and, it is said, so soon as these die, other Moravians are ready to fill their place.—*M'Cheyne's Letters.*

AFAR, 'mid Afric's crimson sands,
  Where skies burn golden down,
And scarce a palm, 'mid thirsty lands,
  Spreads out its fan-leaf crown;
There is a spot of fearful gloom—
  A lazar-house of death—
Where leprosy her living tomb
  Has reared, and held her breath;
As if the Upas' poison shade
Of earth a charnel-vault had made.

No human thing will wander near
  That doleful prison-bound;
No spirit-healer drop a tear
  In that death-haunted ground;

No mother, with unwearied care,
  No leech with healing art,
No Levite, with a balmy prayer
  To chafe the bleeding heart;
No dove, with sprinkled leaf, wings o'er
That shadow, of the dead sea shore.

But there the plague-spot's withering snow,
  Like gangrene eats away,
Ay, inch by inch, with voiceless wo,
  Piece-meal, the mouldering clay;
There, closed within its narrow gate,
  The leper weaves his shroud,
And reads the crisis of his fate,
  Amid the bloated crowd,
Who long for home, yet hopeless weep,
But ne'er return, with weary feet.

O! who will heal the living dead?
  The voice of mercy cries,
And bear to them "the living bread"—
  The "life" that never dies;
"Bind up their wounds" who helpless pine,
  Torn far from home and kin,
And pour love's golden "oil and wine,"
  Their broken hearts within;
Say, who has heard the Saviour's cry,
Who will go in for me and die?

And, who hath crossed that Rubicon,
  Ah! never to return?
Their bosom wrenched from love and home,
  With faith Abra'mic burn;
Say, who hath passed the gate of death,
  Bade earth a long farewell,
Amid the gloom, and fever-breath
  Of dark disease to dwell;
Cut from the heart the tender ties
Of friendship's yearning sympathies?

Two human ones, with God-like love
  For Him who loved them so,
Have followed unto death, to prove
  Compassion's purest glow;
They went, all Saviour-like they went,
  Pure love their only creed;
By no fell persecutor sent
  On torturing rack to bleed—
Not to lift up the battle-cry,
But tell how Christians *do* and die.

Like lamps that light the charnel gloom
  Of some sepulchral shrine,
Doom'd vestals locked in living tomb,
  To trim the lamp divine;
Where never more the voice of friend,
  Nor old "familiar face,"

In life's last hour, may o'er them bend,
  In that death-brooding place,—
Where ne'er again their kindred dear
May wipe away the falling dear.

O ! like earth's veins, a living stream,
  Moravia's sons are found
Wat'ring, all silent and unseen,
  With springs her thirsty ground ;
As streamlets from the stricken rock,
  Their prayers, toil, and tears,
Like tireless waters drop by drop
  Away the mountain wears,—
Whither their hidden channels flow
'Mid Afric's sand or Greenland's snow

LINES,

ON A LETTER FROM DR. DUFF, RELATING THE CONVERSIONS FROM HINDUISM.

GLAD tidings from the burning East afar !
Old Superstition in her temple groans;
The blood-stained wheel of Bumah's idol-car,
That paves its way with human hearts and bones,
Creaks on its rusty axle—and the will
Of the imperial Bramah, child-like, bowed
When "poor Chandala*" whispered "peace, be still,"
And bound the foaming passions of the crowd.—
Behold the still small voice of gospel love
Transmuting eagle natures to the dove !

Hear ye that rich-toned voice, whose master powers
Awake deep echoes in the Christian heart—
Burning from Ind, where triple darkness lowers,
And horrid cruelties hold orgies dark.
From the broad Indian stream, it rushes o'er
"The waste of waters," with no weary tone,
No yearning pinings for his native shore,
But deep heart-pleadings for the Indian lone—
Loud cries that ye may leave your native home,—
"Come o'er and *help* us, *Christian* brethren, *come !*"

*Chandala, a name given to those who have lost caste.

Come ! where the idol gods are gorged with blood,
And Vishnuh feasts on dying "sin-sick" souls—
Where Burragonga's* life-devouring flood,
'Mid the dark shrines of murder, silent rolls.
Come ! where the cloud of immolation's pyre,
Stains the blue heaven with soul polluting rites—
Where blind devotion lights her altar-fire,
O ! bear the gospel's night-dispelling light—
The heathen jungles pierce with clearing beams—
On thirsty deserts pour the living streams.

Come ! with the gospel hammer—strong to break
The stony heart—the hideous idol stones.
Come, trample on the great Goliah's neck,
That strides o'er this "Aceldama" of bones.
O ! gather stones from every brook that flows.
Not in the guided arm the strength is found—
The smallest stone a stripling David throws
May bring the boasting giant to the ground.—
From Nature's darkest ruins, grace can frame
A living temple—to Emmanuel's name !

*Burragonga, the ancient name of the Ganges.

REMEMBRANCE.

When twilight tears are weeping,
O'er closing roses sleeping,
And sudden blasts are sweeping
 The blossom from the tree;
When sad, sad hearts are sighing,
O'er treasured prospects dying,
And silken cords untieing,
 Wilt thou remember me?
When silence deep is stealing,
O'er many a tearful feeling,
And the heart in love is kneeling,
 Wilt thou remember me?

When friends beloved are meeting,
With smiles each other greeting,
And treasured words repeating,
 That marks some hallowed spot;
When heart-born tears are starting,
O'er radiant lights departing,
And clouds and stars are marking,
 Where friends beloved are not;
When hearts are humbly bending,
And holy thoughts ascending,
With burning incense blending,
 Thou wilt not be forgot!

THE END.

CPSIA information can be obtained
at www.ICGtesting.com
Printed in the USA
LVHW100523120522
718524LV00004B/235

9 783375 002169